Liffey Rivers and the Mystery of the Winking Judge

Bronn

Briss

To order additional copies, please contact us.
BookSurge, LLC
www.booksurge.com
1-866-308-6235
orders@booksurge.com

BRENNA
BRIGGS

LIFFEY RIVERS AND THE MYSTERY OF THE WINKING JUDGE

2006

Liffey Rivers and the Mystery of the Winking Judge

ACKNOWLEDGEMENTS

For Rebecca, Maura, Terry and the Skreen, County Sligo, Coffee & Book Clubs, especially Gabrielle and Marguerite

CHAPTER ONE

The almost full suitcase was on the floor next to Liffey Rivers' bed, waiting for her final wardrobe decisions.

The empty solo dress carrier was draped over her desk, like a flabby plastic table cloth.

Liffey was sitting at the desk with last semester's creative writing essays. Red ink circles surrounded many of the words on most of the pages. Liffey was connecting these 'mistake' circles and making them into a slinky.

She was trying to remember how to use *neither* and *nor* and *former* and *latter* and which word was the stupid *former* and which word was the stupid *latter* in sentences. But it was no use. Liffey simply could not get it. And it frustrated her a great deal.

It was almost as frustrating as worrying about when her first solo dress would arrive from Ireland.

Where was the dress?

Liffey decided she had wasted enough time on the slinky. She closed her creative writing notebook, shut down the sentence construction part of her brain, and thought again about how she *really* should have had at *least* a third place in her Open Jig at the Madison Feis.

It was *neither* **fair** *nor* **just** that she had **not even placed**! There! She finally got the 'neither-nor' thing!

She would worry about former and latter later. Like which feis she went to was the *former* and which one was the *latter*.

And which feis she should have never bothered going to in the first place.

Probably she didn't place because she was dancing in the *Open* Jig in her dismal, hideous school dress.

At least she got her usual third and fourth medals in her Novice steps. The good, but-not-good-enough places.

Liffey knew that if she was going to keep progressing in Irish dance competitions, she had to get out of *all* her Novice steps eventually, and into the Open levels of her Reel, Slip Jig, Treble Jig and Hornpipe. So far, she had only reached the Open level in her Soft Shoe Jig. Sometimes, it seemed to Liffey that she would *never* advance in her other steps. It was as difficult as trying to remember if the word *occasion* had one 'c' or two.

When was her solo dress going to get here?

Liffey didn't dare call the dressmaker company in Ireland again. She had called them at least twenty times and had run out of different ways to ask the "Can you *please* tell me *when* I might expect to receive my dress?" question a few weeks ago.

She just wanted to know **WHEN** she could expect to get her dress. Was that so unreasonable? It had been six long weeks now, and Liffey was sick and tired of pretending to be patient.

Liffey was even more sick and tired of trying to be *polite* about it. Operation Solo Dress was not going well.

Maybe she could have her lawyer father call the shop and tell them that it was *illegal* for them to still be working on the Liffey Rivers' dress and that they could be fined up to $5,000.00 or spend six months in jail if Liffey did not get her dress within the next ten days.

Or maybe he could convince them that it was matter of national security that Liffey get her dress right away!

She *had* to think of *something* because she was going crazy waiting for what was going to be the most magnificent dress ever made or worn by anyone, anywhere. Including Cinderella's ball gown and Princess Diana's wedding dress.

She *had* to have her solo dress in time for the Milwaukee Feis in August. She needed to try it out before she and her father went to the most exciting feis of her life in Ireland.

Liffey's father, Robert Rivers, was a prominent criminal defense attorney who often had to travel abroad for legal conferences. Lawyer meetings. Really boring lawyer meetings where "everyone sat around huge conference tables and tried to prove they were important people with important things to say," as her father described them to Liffey.

Liffey had accompanied her father on these trips many times in the past because he did not like leaving her at home with a babysitter after Liffey's mother had died.

They were leaving for London the day after the Milwaukee Feis. Then her father would go to his boring meetings and Liffey would get to go back to the Tower of London and the National Portrait Gallery to see what they looked like, now that she was thirteen.

***

Liffey had visited both places before, when she was ten years old, with a babysitter. She sincerely hoped no one at the Tower of London or National Portrait Gallery would remember what she looked like.

"Maybe I should dye my hair black or metallic purple," Liffey thought, remembering how humiliated she had been when one of the Tower guards insisted she get off the Crown Jewel People Mover. He had made her stand right next to him, red faced, until that ditzy nanny-sitter found her forty-five minutes later.

And *then*, later the *same* day, her father, Scotland Yard and probably the *entire* staff at the National Portrait Gallery, had combed the art gallery searching for her after she had again dodged the nanny.

Pink hair would be too much. Red or blue might work. Not orange though. Orange might cause people to stare at her.

***

It had been three nights now without the screaming dreams, and Liffey was confident she could sleep all the way through the night again. All she had to do was say her night prayers, say goodnight to her mother in heaven and picture the Crown Jewels of England in their display cases, sparkling like the Milky Way does on really clear nights.

CHAPTER TWO

L iffey was beginning to lose interest in doing the *Titanic* 'Rose and Jack' scene on the prow of the ship. She had been standing in the rain now, arms outstretched on the top deck of an empty, open air, double-decker London tour bus for about twenty minutes as it raced around Hyde Park. She did not care if people stared and pointed at her from the heavy traffic below as her iPod played the broken heart song over and over.

Liffey really wished she could stand facing *forward*, which was the correct way to do the scene. But there was a problem with facing forward at the front of this bus because there was a huge windshield which ruined the whole mood of pretending to be on the prow of the boat with the wind slapping her face. So Liffey stood facing *backwards* instead and it worked just fine until the lightly falling rain began to form little water pellets which began to sting her eyelids and nose.

Reluctantly, Liffey started down the steep stairs of the bus, grabbing on to the railing as it lurched forward.

"I'll get off at Trafalgar Square and climb up one of the lions," she decided, remembering how exhilarating it had been to jump into one of the fountains at Trafalgar on a sweltering August day three years ago.

***

Liffey was still worried about being recognized at the

National Portrait Gallery, even though it had been 1,095 days since the nanny incident. She had scratched the idea of coloring her hair to make sure no one would recognize her because her father would ask a million questions and probably not permit her to keep the color anyway. Instead, she brought with her a pair of large, non-prescription glasses to quickly put on if any of the guards seemed to look at her twice like they might have seen her before. She was also wearing a reversible jacket.

Liffey had enjoyed going through the Tudor Gallery when she was ten with its portraits of kings and queens wearing their jewels as casually as Liffey wore her track pants to and from her Irish dance classes.

She had especially liked the Queen Elizabeth I portraits. Liffey had never seen so many jewels on anyone. Pearls were sprinkled all over the queen's gowns like confetti.

Robert Rivers had hired a Mary Poppins named Edna from a nanny agency to entertain Liffey while he went to meetings. After the Tower of London mishap, Edna and Liffey went directly to the National Portrait Gallery in a huge black London taxi cab to look at portraits of queens and kings.

In the Tudor Gallery, Liffey decided to count the number of jewels in the Queen Elizabeth I portraits. Probably no one had ever done that before and she thought that it would be far less boring than making the rounds with toady Edna looking at dead people's portraits and listening to Edna saying weird things like "you can buy fresh beet root in Portobello Road."

Liffey did not even know what fresh beet root was. Or why it would be in the road.

As soon as they had arrived, Liffey convinced Edna to go for tea downstairs and then ditched the nanny for the rest of the afternoon.

Later, she would tell a very angry Robert Rivers that she

did *not* actually *hide* from the nanny. As Liffey described it, the nanny had simply *forgotten* what Liffey looked like. Her father never quite believed this version of Liffey's great escape, but it was more-or-less true.

In retrospect, Liffey was aware at the time that it had been unkind to ignore poor Edna, who was obviously very distressed that this time she actually *had* lost her charge. She rushed frantically by Liffey several times as Liffey systematically counted the jewels in the Queen Elizabeth I portraits.

Some nanny! Edna did not even *recognize* her. She went back and forth right in front of Liffey muttering, "Little girl, little girl, where are you?"

Liffey *refused* to look the deranged woman in the eye because she *plainly* heard Edna calling: *"Shannon, Shannon, where are you, dear?"*

The river thing again. It was *always* the same. No one *ever* remembered the name of the girl who was named after that river in Ireland.

***

At least now that she was thirteen, Liffey was allowed to go places by herself. No more nannies to dodge.

Liffey tried to look nonchalant as she entered the National Portrait Gallery. She walked up the main entrance stairs past two security guards, who did not seem to notice her at all, and into the Tudor Gallery.

Passing by a large, gloomy group portrait of what was labeled the 'More' family, Liffey locked eyes with a portrait of Queen Anne Boleyn and admired the 'B' ornament she wore on the necklace around her famous neck.

"Ugh," thought Liffey, "This is the head that Henry the Eighth paid a French swordsman to cut off."

The way Liffey understood this ghastly deed, was that because Anne had given birth to a baby *girl*, who turned out to be Queen Elizabeth I, and the baby *boy* she had given birth to died, King Henry VIII decided he had better get another wife to try for a baby boy.

Apparently, Henry could not even *imagine* a girl running England. Like there was something *wrong* with a girl being in charge of a country! Like it was Anne Boleyn's *fault* that the baby boy had died and she could not produce another one. So he made up treason lies about Anne and got rid of her.

Henry had already discarded his first wife, Queen Catherine of Aragon, when she, like Anne Boleyn, had only managed to have a baby girl, the future Queen Mary Tudor. Liffey thought it was great that the *two girls* had managed to become queens of England after all, in spite of Henry VIII's stupid attempts to prevent such a thing. "Girl power," smiled Liffey.

Liffey felt disgusted and sad as she studied this Anne Boleyn portrait. It was completed before Anne Boleyn knew what her fate would be at the Tower of London. There was a little Mona Lisa kind of smile on her face which seemed to say "I'm the Queen of England and everything is perfect." Liffey's father told her that Anne Boleyn's motto on her official queen medal had been 'The moost happi.' Liffey was not sure if the queen had trouble spelling like she herself did, or if they just spelled words differently back then.

Shaking her head, thinking that "boys were just as stupid in Anne Boleyn's time as they were now," Liffey moved on, passing by yet *another* one of King Henry VIII's wives, Catherine Parr.

Liffey recalled that this controversial king had had *six wives*. He either divorced them, beheaded them or they were lucky enough to die naturally or outlive him. She could remember them in order with a rhyme her father had taught her long ago: "Divorced, Beheaded, Died. Divorced, Beheaded, Survived."

Liffey was startled to notice that Queen Catherine Parr was wearing an incredible crown. *How* had she missed that when she was here before? It had *definite* solo dress crown possibilities. "I think this is the queen who survived," Liffey determined, making a mental note to get a postcard of Catherine Parr downstairs in the gift shop for future solo dress crown ideas.

Moving away from Queen Catherine, Liffey barely noticed the boring paintings of church officials and noblemen and other very dead, dull-looking people she saw hanging on the walls.

Then she saw the *huge* painting of Henry VIII and shuddered. She could not even look at him or his small son standing next to him without thinking about Anne Boleyn's head lying on Tower Green.

Liffey remembered that the Henry VIII wife who finally had the *boy* kind of baby for him was Jane Seymour. Jane died at Hampton Court of childbirth fever shortly after she gave birth to the future King Edward VI, who died when he was only 15 years old.

When Liffey toured the palace at Hampton Court where Henry had lived with some of his queens, the tour guide told them stories about how the ghost of Jane Seymour was sometimes seen running like a madwoman along the hallways and down the stairs into the palace kitchen.

This had interested Liffey a great deal and she had seriously considered ditching her father and hiding out at Hampton Court that night to see if Jane Seymour's ghost came running by, but had decided that after all the trouble she had caused at the Tower of London and National Portrait Gallery, she had better not. Even the incredible patience her father had for Liffey's misadventures was more or less worn out by Hampton Court time.

Still hiding out at Hampton Court remained high on Liffey's lists of things to do, because there were *other* ghost stories about *another* one of Henry's wives who had lived there too. Her name was Catherine Howard.

The Catherine Howard ghost tales recounted the young queen sobbing and screaming as she ran through the haunted gallery towards the palace chapel. Catherine's ghost was seen pounding on the doors of the chapel, *begging* Henry for mercy before he had her shipped to the Tower to be beheaded. Liffey's father told her that there were no portraits of twenty-two-year-old Queen Catherine Howard because Henry probably had them all destroyed after he had her head cut off. Robert Rivers said it was the 'out-of-sight, out-of-mind' rule.

And what was even *better* than screaming queen ghosts, Liffey had read an article *recently* about an image of a man ghost captured on security *video tape* at Hampton Court. The article said that a palace door had been mysteriously *unbolted* several times during a period of weeks after having been locked by security staff at night. Special cameras had been set up to catch whoever was doing the unlocking and the video tape showed a man wearing *period dress* of Henry VIII's court!

Liffey was *sure* she would see something too if she could only figure out how to convince her father to leave her there. Since she had only been ten years old at the time, and after the art gallery and Tower incidents, her father was not letting Liffey out of his sight. Some day Liffey fully intended to find a way to meet the ghosts at Hampton Court.

CHAPTER THREE

Liffey continued focusing her thirteen-year-old eyes on royal Tudor portraits. The first Queen Elizabeth I portrait Liffey spotted was the one with the big crown. It was by far the simplest painting in the gallery for pearl and jewel counting because first of all, there were not a zillion precious stones on it like there were on most of Elizabeth's other portraits, and secondly, the jewels were pretty much organized into specific places on the queen's coronation robe.

Liffey called this 'Crowning Portrait' the 'Wee Willie Winkie Elizabeth' because she had used that nursery rhyme to count the pearls on the chain of jewels which was draped over the queen's ermine cape.

Liffey had invented a counting system using nursery rhymes when she was in the second grade and completely bored with numbers.

It had always been much easier for Liffey to work with words than numbers. If she used her favorite nursery rhymes to count things instead of numbers, she could remember something forever.

The 'Wee Willie Winkie' ryhme had 43 syllables and there were 43 'Winkie' pearls on the long chain of jewels that held the queen's ermine coronation robe together. Liffey had spent a great deal of time figuring out how many things she could remember using the number 43 because the Winkie rhyme was her favorite and she liked to apply it to as many things as she could.

Sometimes it paid off. Liffey could immediately say '43' when her teacher asked her class last year, "How many presidents of the United States have there been so far?" After the next election of course, the Winkie rhyme would *not* work for the president count. But Liffey was the only one in the class that could spit that number out last quarter and it was only because of the Winkie rhyme.

She memorized other number 43 Winkie facts as well in case she ever would have the opportunity to impress anyone.

For instance, Liffey knew that 'technetium' was the name of the atomic number 43. That fact might come in handy in high school if she took chemistry.

And the direct dial code for Austria was also the number 43. If anyone ever came up to her and said "I wonder how to call Austria?" Liffey would be ready with the reply, "first, you dial 43."

But the *best* Winkie 43 fact to remember was that Gimli the dwarf had killed 43 enemies at the Battle of the Hornburg.

***

Liffey scrutinized this portrait of the young Queen Elizabeth I with its white onion skin tone. Comparing it with the portraits in the gallery of an older Queen Elizabeth I, with their dull eyes and blood-drained appearance, Liffey considered the idea that the Goth look might have originated with Queen Elizabeth I. Queen Elizabeth I might have actually *invented* the Goth look. Of course no historian would *dare* to suggest such a thing, but Liffey thought perhaps the time had come to investigate such a possibility. She added analyzing the 'Elizabeth-Goth' connection, along with the ghosts of Hampton Court, on her extensive list of things to do.

Liffey however, did not really care much about whether or not the queen was a Goth, or how dismal Queen Elizabeth's complexion was because what the queen's skin lacked in luster, was more than made up for by the pearls and jewels on her spectacular gowns! There were pearls and more pearls and rubies and onyx and diamonds and emeralds all over the royal dresses and robes the queen wore in her portraits.

Concentrating now on the Crowning Portrait, Liffey began to count the pearls which bordered the queen's chain of precious stones:

'**Wee Wil-lie Wink-ie runs through the town, up-stairs and down-stairs in his night-gown. Tap-ping at the win-dow and cry-ing through the lock, are all the child-ren in their beds it's past eight-o'-clock?**'

Liffey gasped. Something was *WRONG*! There seemed to be an *extra pearl* left over *after* the 43 Winkie syllables were counted. She had just counted 44 pearls! How could that be? There *had* to be 43 pearls! She had used her scientific rhyme counting system three years ago and it was foolproof. She was *positive* that there were 43 border pearls on the queen's chain. There were also nine large drop pearls attached to the sash and Liffey remembered them because a cat has nine lives.

Liffey was *sure* she had used the Winkie rhyme to count the pearls on this chain.

Liffey decided to have another go at the pearl count. She breathed in deeply, tried to collect herself and counted again. There was still an *extra* pearl! There was no doubt whatsoever that there were *44 pearls*! Just as Liffey was beginning to think that she must have made a mistake because she had only been ten years old at the time of the first count, she felt a little pinprick at the bottom of her neck like the static electricity shock you get in the dry winter air when you touch someone or try to comb your hair.

Liffey was apprehensive. "Not here. Not now." Were these the warning prickles she would often get if she were in danger? How could Queen Elizabeth I's portrait place her in any kind of *danger*?

Liffey tried to will the prickly sensations away but they were beginning to feel like the stabbing pellets of rain that had driven Liffey down from the upper deck of the tour bus earlier today. They hurt. Then Liffey felt the all too familiar warning creepy crawly pins and needles running up and down her entire spine telling her that something was definitely *wrong* with this portrait.

There was *one extra pearl* on the chain. Liffey was *sure* of it! The Winkie rhyme had worked perfectly the *first* time she had tried it three years ago. She was so totally sure because usually in order to get a 'fit' for a rhyme, several rhymes had to be tried before one would fit. Sometimes, Liffey even ended up cheating a little and adding or subtracting a syllable or two to make a rhyme fit to what she was counting. That was why she was *so positive* that something was *wrong* with this Crowning Portrait. Winkie had been a *perfect fit* the first time!

Suddenly, the pins and needles felt like an electric circuit shock surging through her and Liffey *knew* what was wrong. *This portrait was a fake*! The *real* painting must have been stolen and this one put in its place!

Liffey glanced around her and had absolutely no clue what to do. Who would believe a thirteen-year-old girl's story that one of the most prominent paintings in the National Portrait Gallery of the United Kingdom was a *fake*? She knew that there was no one who would believe her. Especially since the name

'Liffey Rivers' had to be in the 'Who's Who of Troublemakers' files at this place.

***

Liffey cringed, remembering how she had to sit in the gallery director's office while her father explained that his ten-year-old daughter had not really gone missing in the gallery and how sorry he was that his daughter had caused such chaos.

Edna, the nanny, had completely over-reacted and had actually called Scotland Yard *before* she had notified Mr. Rivers that his daughter was missing. By the time the panicked Robert Rivers had arrived at the National Portrait Gallery, it was like a zoo. There were police detectives and gallery security and Edna in tears blowing her nose into a handkerchief. Mechanically, Robert Rivers had pulled a photo of Liffey out of his wallet for the detectives and immediately went on his own search even though they urged him to remain calm and to sit down.

It took him approximately thirty seconds to locate Liffey. She was standing right at the top of the stairs, not very far into the Tudor Gallery, counting (for the third time) the pearls on Queen Elizabeth I's Crowning Portrait. He was flabbergasted.

"Liffey Rivers," he practically shouted. "What in the world is going on here?"

Liffey tried to explain to her father that Edna did not even know what she looked like because she had passed by her at least fifteen times.

"And you didn't *tell* the poor woman who you were?" "No, Daddy. I did *not*. She kept calling out for a '*Shannon*' and as you of all people know *very* well, I am *not* named after *that* river."

Mr. Roberts went on. "And I suppose you did not *notice* the police and gallery guards searching for you either?"

"*They* were calling for a 'Shannon' too. How should I know that they meant Liffey?"

Liffey knew that was kind of a smart-aleck remark to make to her father but she did not know what else to say. She waited for a tirade about how *could* she, but instead her father let out a loud *laugh*. Liffey had feared when he arrived that he might actually spank her right on the spot even though he had never done that before. But he had *laughed*. Liffey wondered if that was what 'hysteria' was. She had seen people in movies laughing or screaming when they really should have been crying about something. Her father must have been hysterical.

CHAPTER FOUR

Mr. Smith sat staring out from compartment B's window, his mind racing along at the speed of the train which was still one hour north of Paddington Station.

This plan was flawless. It would work without any glitches. But the doubts lingered. After all, it had been a 13-year-old Irish dancer who had outsmarted him in St. Louis only a few months ago and he had lost the biggest client he had ever had because he had failed to deliver those diamonds.

Mr. Smith's confidence level was definitely at low tide. And his ex-girlfriend had probably told the Feds everything by now. It was a miracle he had not been picked up yet.

"Liffey Rivers," he grunted. "What kind of name is *that* anyway?"

"Well, this plan is already in motion," he reminded himself, and the "odds of running into that little wig-head again are one in a billion." He was confident that she would never recognize him even if their paths did happen to cross again someday. He smiled to himself, finally taking in the English countryside. It was going to be a beautiful day. Absolutely flawless.

CHAPTER FIVE

L iffey wanted to scream out "Help! Help!"

But would this even 'technically' be considered an emergency? How did a 13-year-old sound the 'alarm' that a valuable national treasure had been stolen? "There really is no simple way to do this," Liffey thought. "I will have to act very casual, like it is really no big deal that a famous painting has been stolen, or no one will listen to me. I cannot act as crazy and freaked-out as I feel."

"I will start by telling one of those stiff-jawed guards at the door that there is a *slight* problem. Maybe I should yawn when I tell them the news, like, even though it is a fake, it's really no big deal. I just thought they maybe ought to know a national treasure has gone missing, since they are the people who are supposed to be guarding the stuff."

Liffey toyed with the idea of calling her father out of his late morning meeting for some advice, but after the previous catastrophe at the gallery three years ago, she *really* wanted to keep him out of any new gallery dramas. She would just tell the guards and then move on to the modern portraits and let things take their course.

***

"Well, here goes nothing," thought Liffey as she tried to make up her mind which guard she should tell about the fake painting of Queen Elizabeth I.

She had two choices. There was the cute, young-looking guard who obviously knew how good looking he was because he was posing beside the door like a male model, and there was an older, smug-looking, bald security guard.

Undoubtedly, the bald guard had to be more experienced and Liffey had no idea how many, if any, famous portraits had ever gone missing from the National Portrait Gallery before. Probably none. Although Liffey had heard that a famous portrait of Princess Diana had sort of gone missing, so it must be a somewhat familiar topic around the gallery. Everybody acted like the Diana painting was *not* missing but nobody seemed to know exactly what had *happened* to it. She wanted the Queen Elizabeth I Crowning Portrait mystery to be taken seriously.

It also seemed logical to her that an older man might be less likely to over-react to such news. He would probably just nod his bald head, take her statement, and then tell her she was free to go and that he would handle everything. Of course he would thank her for her amazing observation and tell her that the gallery would let her know when they solved the mystery. Yes. Liffey would tell the bald guard.

Liffey Rivers walked slowly over to the bald security guard, who looked tired and disinterested in his surroundings, and tried to deliver the disturbing news. "The loo is downstairs, young lady," he informed Liffey before she could even get one word out of her mouth. This caught Liffey off-guard. What was a 'loo' anyway? And why did he think she wanted one?

Liffey smiled weakly and said "Thank-you, sir, that's nice." The bald man grunted. Liffey tried to continue but the guard again spoke up saying, "well then, the cafeteria and gift shop are down two flights of stairs as well."

"That's nice," Liffey said again. "Actually, sir, I need to tell you about a problem with one of your portraits."

The bald guard fairly barked back at Liffey that he was not an artist and if she thought one of the portraits had something wrong with it, she should discuss it with her art teacher.

This sounding-the-alarm thing was not going well.

"No wonder Paul Revere used a *horse* to help him sound *his* alarm," Liffey thought. No one would have listened to him if he had just politely walked up to them and tried to *tell* them the British were coming! Liffey, however, could not quite see herself running around the National Portrait Gallery yelling "To search! To search! Queen Elizabeth the First has gone missing!" So she tried one more time.

"Sir, I *mean* that the Crowning Portrait of Queen Elizabeth I is a *fake*!"

This startling revelation caused the guard to look Liffey directly in the eye and raise one of his eyebrows quizzically. Liffey held his gaze and continued: "There are too many pearls on her chain."

"I see," said the bald guard. "And just *how* do you know that?" he asked.

"Because there are 43 syllables in the Wee Willie Winkie rhyme. I used it to count the pearls on the chain three years ago when I was here before. *Now* the Winkie rhyme does not fit. The word 'clock' should have been the last pearl. *That* means that there is one more pearl today than there was three years ago in August."

"Right-o," said the bald guard, obviously doing his best not to laugh out loud at Liffey's revelation. "I will let Sherlock Holmes know immediately and I am sure he will put this in order. Thank you so much for your help. Her Majesty will be most grateful."

Liffey could tell she was not going to get anywhere with this man, who was obviously not taking her seriously, and that if she continued to explain things, he would probably start roaring with laughter. He had already walked away from Liffey over to the cute guard at the other door and they were both smiling at her now.

She needed *proof*. Her lawyer father was always saying things like: "Show me the *proof*. Where's the *evidence?*"

Liffey would have to *get* the proof. She could not just keep explaining the Winkie ryhme *over* and *over* to adults all day. They would just keep laughing at her. Liffey suddenly realized that she *could* get the evidence she needed to sound the alarm. "I need a postcard or poster of the *real portrait* and then I can *compare* it with the fake painting!" thought Liffey. "I completely *forgot* to do the thinking cap trick before I talked to that smug old man."

Liffey's father had taught her to do the 'thinking cap trick' when she was afraid of or baffled by someone or something. It was a survival game she had learned when she was very young. In difficult moments of fear or indecision, Liffey was to imagine that she had dropped her thinking cap. She would then bend down, pick it up and put it back on her head. The trick usually worked and helped Liffey to think clearly again.

Liffey was grateful that at least in *this* particular case, she did not seem to be in any danger. How *could* she be? She was fairly certain that the warning pins and needles had only been alerting her to the fact that something was very *wrong* with the Queen Elizabeth I portrait. Still, it made her think twice because they had been so intense.

With the thinking cap in place again, Liffey decided that there was no rush to buy the poster or post card and get back to the security guards with her evidence. "Let them have a good laugh up there," she thought. "I need to calm down a little if

I am ever to successfully convince them that the Crowning Portrait is a fake."

Liffey headed down the stairs through the bricked arches into the Portrait Cafe. Everywhere she looked there were books and posters and postcards and more books. Liffey was hungry and determined. "I will feed my brain and then go back upstairs and *prove* my case." Food first. Then get the evidence.

Moving into the cafeteria-style food area, Liffey picked up a tray and studied the menu written on a chalk board. She tried to imagine eating a goat's cheese quiche, then stopped and tried not to giggle when she saw 'petite torte-eaters.' She wished her father could see this. Liffey knew that the word 'tort' without the 'e' at the end in law books meant something like 'negligent,' or bad things you did that were not criminal acts but still caused people a lot of trouble. Her father always said that 'Tort' should have been Liffey's middle name.

She opted for the goat's cheese quiche because it sounded sophisticated. She also selected a cup of tea to complete the sophisticated mood.

The quiche was delicious and gave Liffey some much needed energy to begin scouring the gift shop for Queen Elizabeth I posters. Liffey was delighted that the third group of historical posters she looked at were all about the queen. She heard herself crying out "yeeees!" when she spotted a booklet stuffed with large posters of important portraits of Queen Elizabeth I. The cover art on the booklet was the *real* Crowning Portrait. Or was it? What if the poster was created *after* the switch? She would have to assume that it was *not* and then do more research.

Liffey could almost not believe her good fortune! Even though the price tag was a bit expensive, she eagerly paid the clerk and went back to her unfinished tea and opened the poster packet.

What she needed was some *vocabulary* other than the 'Winkie pearl talk' if she was *ever* going to get anyone to listen to her story. First she needed to examine the poster. Then she would compare it with the portrait upstairs in the Tudor Gallery to figure out where the extra pearl was located. It was time to do a Winkie pearl count on the poster.

"*Yes!*" It fit perfectly. Liffey was ecstatic that the count was 43 pearls! All Liffey needed to do now was to take it upstairs and find the *extra pearl* on the *fake* portrait! She would try the cute guard this time and see if she could convince him that something was *very* wrong with the Crowning Portrait.

As she studied the booklet and Crowning Portrait poster, Liffey learned that the gold embroidered collar which reached all the way up to and actually covered the queen's ears was called a "ruff." "Whatever," Liffey snickered, wondering what it would be like to say to someone: "Do you like my ruff?"

Liffey read that the wide necklace around the queen's neck was logically called a collar.

Then Liffey found out that the 'Winkie count pearls' were on what she herself had already called the 'chain' because it *looked* like a chain!

There. As her father would say, "You have the right words. Now form them into cold, hard evidence."

Liffey gulped the last sip of what was now cold tea and tried to mentally prepare herself for round two of the Wee Willie Winkie pearl riddle.

***

Mr. Smith was hungry and he needed to clear his head.

"Train rides are draining," he thought as he punched his ticket through the automated turnstiles.

Paddington Station was a madhouse with people running for trains they had probably already missed and others looking at overhead schedules. He could not believe how many stuffed Paddington Bears and books were on display. "*Who* would want to read a book about a bear wandering all over London?"

Mr. Smith preferred 'how to do it yourself' and 'practical advice' books. Books about carpentry and art were on his hot list now.

He walked briskly towards the main exit and spotted a taxi pulling up. By sheer luck it was not occupied. As he opened the door and tossed in his light-weight luggage, he again thought about what a flawless day it had been. "With many more to come," he assured himself, nervously running his fingers through his wavy, snow white hair.

CHAPTER SIX

It was a long, long walk back up the stairs into the Tudor Gallery.

Liffey looked for the guards when she reached the top of the landing but they did not seem to be around. This was good, because Liffey needed to compare the poster of Queen Elizabeth I she was carrying with the *fake* portrait hanging on the wall and find pearl # 44. She was relieved to realize that she would not be laughed at by the guards while she was doing the comparison work.

Liffey had folded the poster so she could easily hold it up in front of the portrait on the wall and do the count. She began with the outside pearl on her right which was the queen's left shoulder.

"Good ghillies!" Liffey was astonished! Why had no one noticed this *obvious extra* pearl before now? It was *so obvious* it was almost ridiculous!

Without even having to do the Winkie rhyme count *one* time, Liffey could plainly *see* that the extra pearl was the fourth one from the queen's right shoulder.

The *real* Crowning Portrait had a large *gap* where fake pearl # 44 was now inserted. The fake painting actually looked more balanced than the real portrait!

Liffey looked carefully and saw that what the copy cat artist had *not* observed was that there were three pearls above and below each of the square pieces of onyx on the queen's chain. The art forger had done an incredible job and then apparently let his or her own sense of perfection try to *improve* the Crowning Portrait by adding the pearl! And it seemed that so far, only thirteen-year-old Liffey Rivers had noticed!

Liffey's heart was pounding and her mouth was dry. This was definitely "cold, hard evidence," she thought. She looked again at the queen's eyes. They reminded Liffey of turtle eyes. No eye lashes. No expression. She had seen eyes like those before on an elevator in St. Louis. And in the screaming dreams.

CHAPTER SEVEN

Now that Liffey had the *proof* she needed to take to the security guards (who still were not at their posts), she contemplated whether they were even the right people to tell in the first place.

They might choose not believe her because they probably would not want to deal with it. Or, they might act interested and then never even *tell* the National Portrait Gallery officials what Liffey had discovered, thinking it would be for the greater good of everyone *not* to divulge Liffey's discovery. She knew she was only a little girl in their eyes, and even if what she pointed out to them *looked* suspicious, they might think that there had to be a logical explanation for the extra pearl and decide to keep it to themselves. Liffey did not want to risk this. She thought again about contacting her father, but could not shake off the humiliation from her previous visit three years ago.

A woman.

Liffey needed to find a *woman* guard who would not laugh at her. Or maybe one of the women tour guides she had seen leading children around the gallery. They were used to stupid questions and probably would not immediately dismiss Liffey if she approached them and told them what she had discovered. Certainly a guide would not initially believe her, *but* if she could get the guide to come into the Tudor Gallery with her, then maybe she could make her point and get some adult assistance.

Unless. And this "unless" was another message from her father's "how life works when the ego is compromised list." *Unless*, no one who worked with the Gallery would *want* anyone on the outside world to find out about the fraud Liffey had uncovered inside the National Portrait Gallery!

Before Liffey could decide who *should* know about the fake portrait and who should *not*, she felt a light tap on her right shoulder. She glanced quickly around and saw it was the cute, young guard.

Liffey tried hard not to choke. This guard was movie star material and Liffey was rendered speechless by his good looks and cool and casual manner. She *had* to keep her focus. He was obviously just trying to be nice. He probably knew that she knew the guards had been making fun of her. And they *had* hurt her feelings. Liffey also knew that what was really important here now, was that someone be alerted as to what had happened to Queen Elizabeth I's portrait. Liffey had *proof* that this portrait of Queen Elizabeth I was a *fake*. How much *bigger* could something get?

She felt herself melting when he smiled at her and asked "So, what's up, Luv?"

She wanted to tell him everything about herself and her Irish dancing and her dog and even the problem with Queen Elizabeth I's Crowning Portrait.

"What's your name, Luv?" he asked with his lethal charm. Liffey tried to remember. She *knew* she *knew* the answer, but it was buried deep inside her somewhere.

As she frantically stammered trying to say something, *anything*, she heard what she later believed to be her own voice saying: "Do you know they sell fresh beet root in Portobello Road?"

CHAPTER EIGHT

Before Liffey could die of embarrassment, she was saved by a passing tour group of what appeared to be four or five-year-olds. They barged right into her to get close to the Crowning Portrait of Queen Elizabeth I which Liffey was now unintentionally blocking from public view.

The love of her life smiled a little confusedly at Liffey and then backed away from the noisy children into the doorway of the Tudor Gallery entrance.

Still stunned by her tongue tied swoon, Liffey tried to regain her composure. She was standing in a sea of wriggling, giggling preschoolers. Their guide, or docent, was an older woman, probably a retired teacher who was now a gallery volunteer. "You couldn't *pay* anyone enough to take this underage group of shrieking children through an art gallery," Liffey thought. This guide *had* to be a volunteer.

Liffey was too upset to move away from the crowd. "How *could* I have heard Edna's beet root blabber coming out of my own mouth?" she asked herself over and over. She was afraid she might *never* be able to tell a cute boy her name ever again. "Maybe I should wear a name tag like these little blobs. Then I don't have to risk opening my stupid mouth."

The self-pity Liffey was drowning in was suddenly replaced with a tinge of interest. Did she hear the tour guide telling these tots that the *original* Crowning Portrait had been *lost* hundreds of years ago and that this one was more or less recreated from *memory* hundreds of years ago? "No way," Liffey cried out. *"So this fake is a copy of a copy?"*

The tour guide quizzed her little group: "Why was the original Crowning Portrait recreated from *memory?*" Liffey almost raised her hand to answer "because they did not have cameras then," but remembered she was thirteen just in time to spare herself from more humiliation. She let the five-year-olds have a go at the answer. None of them seemed able to come up with the word 'camera' though, and finally the tour guide gave up.

The children were crabby and loud and did not seem to be in the least bit interested. The tour guide looked exhausted. Liffey wondered how many other portraits this poor woman had tried to introduce to these obviously disinterested children today. "Maybe I can cheer her up with my Winkie pearl discovery. She would probably be amazed that the *copy* of the original portrait that got lost has now been replaced with another *copy!*"

The tour guide was holding her hands over her ears trying to block out the piercing chatter of the junior infants tour.

This was Liffey's opportunity to tell the tour guide about the fake portrait. She maneuvered through the tots, looked into the tour guide's glazed over eyes, and blurted out that she had discovered an amazing *recent* forgery of this very Crowning Portrait! The tour guide, who seemed shell shocked and distant, responded: "That's nice, dear."

"This woman is in way over her head with these tots," Liffey concluded. She would have to figure out someone else to tell about the switch, which brought her back to the cute guard. But *how* could she *ever* face him again after the 'Portobello Road fresh beet root' catastrophe? She couldn't.

Dejectedly, Liffey sat down on a bench in the long Tudor

Gallery directly in front of another painting of Queen Elizabeth I, called the 'Ditchley Portrait.' She had never finished counting the pearls and rubies on this masterpiece. There were just too many to know where to begin, even if she used a rhyme. The Ditchley Portrait suited her mood at the moment. It was dark and moody and Queen Elizabeth I looked like a sorceress with bolts of lightning behind her.

Liffey entertained the idea that maybe *this* portrait was a phony one too. Maybe they *all* were! Maybe one person had single handedly wiped out the *entire* National Portrait Gallery's collection of Queen Elizabeth I portraits and was now using the real ones as dart boards like the Joker might do in a *Batman* story.

***

Liffey could feel herself retreating into her solo dress brain, the safe little place where she would go to regroup when things around her got to be too much. She imagined herself now on a feis stage in Ireland wearing the shimmering blue solo dress she was *finally* going to pick up in Dublin on the way to the Beltra Feis.

Liffey's dress, as she had carefully planned, would be one-of-a-kind. Liffey had used ancient Celtic Ogham alphabet markings inside the Celtic rope design on her dress. They spelled out her last name: R-I-V-E-R-S. Liffey was absolutely positive that the feiseanna adjudicators would have no clue that she was breaking *every feis rule* there was standing brazenly before them wearing her *name* in plain view above the cardboard number tied around her waist!

To make sure that in the unlikely case that an adjudicator *did* know the Ogham alphabet, like from genetic memory or something, Liffey had put the Ogham marks design into a coded message. Ogham is written from either bottom to top or from right to left. The name R-I-V-E-R-S, spelled from left to right as it was on Liffey's solo dress, would only spell out 'Rivers' *if* an adjudicator broke the code and watched Liffey dance using a MIRROR when the name would be reversed! Ogham had become Liffey's private alphabet. She liked to think of herself as an Oghamologist. Like there were Egyptologists.

***

Liffey's blue solo dress moment ended abruptly when the horde of junior infants descended upon the Queen Elizabeth I Ditchley Portrait. Liffey looked into their little beady eyeballs, which were level were her own now from her bench sitting position. "Cute, but no thanks," she thought to herself. She wondered if she had been such a loud mouth when she was five. The tour guide arrived behind them, totally out of gas.

Liffey was afraid the docent might not have the strength left to complete her tour with the children. The guide placed herself in front of the portrait's lightning bolts, smiled weakly, and then burst into tears!

Liffey stood up concerned. The junior infants didn't even seem to notice that their guide was crying right in front of them. "They have not been listening to the docent at all from the very beginning of their tour," Liffey realized, deciding to take matters into her own hands.

She would take the children *back* to the Crowning Portrait and do the Winkie rhyme with them and tell them about the extra pearl! Their guide was obviously having a nervous breakdown and this would give the guide a moment to relax *and* give Liffey a chance to practice speaking publicly about the art theft.

So far, Liffey had not been able to get *any* adults to listen to her. Maybe the under-six crowd would find it interesting.

CHAPTER NINE

With the best of intentions, Liffey walked up to the docent and took over.

"Hello boys and girls! Guess what? I know a secret! It's in a painting right across the room! Would you like to come with me to see it? There is an *extra pearl* in the picture and I will show you how to find it." The children continued their screeching. No one bothered to look up at Liffey.

Liffey picked up her volume: "Look guys, this is *serious*! It's an *emergency*!"

The word 'emergency' had an immediate effect on the children.

There was a hush and then complete silence.

In a very orderly fashion, they formed themselves into a line and began to walk towards the 'Way Out' sign with great dignity.

This was not at all what Liffey had intended! The children were heading for the *exit* holding hands in a long chain. They had obviously had extensive training for possible emergency situations.

The docent, seeing her charges walking away in an emergency formation line, grabbed the large whistle around her neck and shoved it into her mouth. The shrill short blasts from the whistle caused the children to move faster and the docent to blow louder.

This was beginning to cause major ripples throughout

the Tudor Gallery. Visitors were looking around wildly for the source of the problem. Was there a fire? A bomb threat?

Liffey sat down again in front of the Ditchley Portrait watching helplessly as the situation accelerated into an even higher gear. She could not *believe* what was going on!

Just when she thought things could not get any worse, she heard a deafening fire alarm siren. It was one of those gulping kind of sirens that makes terrifying noise like in submarine movies when the sub has to dive under water because an airplane was going to blow it up. The Tudor Gallery had turned into an impending disaster scene!

Liffey tried hard not to blame herself. *How* could she have anticipated that the goofy docent was going to start blowing an alarm whistle?

And *who* had set off the *fire alarm?*

Outside the gallery, Liffey thought she heard fire engines approaching. "Time to go," Liffey decided. It sounded like the entire London fire fighting brigade was en route.

Suddenly, Liffey had an idea. An inspiration really.

If she did *not* leave, and went back to the Crowing Portrait and just *stayed* there, sooner or later some kind of an official would have to come by and then she could expose the forgery. Liffey thought it was worth a try. She was beginning to feel desperate. She was leaving for Ireland the next morning and if she did not point out this problem today, she did not know when she would ever get back to London again to handle it.

The Tudor Gallery appeared to be empty as she made her way back to the Crowning Portrait. The translucent face of Queen Elizabeth I staring at her looked whiter than ever. Liffey noticed the little blue veins on the queen's forehead. She looked so fragile. Liffey knew, however, that Elizabeth I had ruled for over forty years, so she could not have been nearly as delicate as she appeared to be in this painting.

There were pounding feet. Police were streaming into the gallery followed by a huge group of firemen. The siren was still screaming its eardrum-bursting warning.

Liffey stood her ground. She folded her arms and prepared for the confrontation.

It came.

"Out! Everybody *out*, please! Come on, miss, follow me now because we have to *leave* the gallery. There's an emergency situation going on. That's a good girl."

Liffey faced the 'out please' policeman and spoke slowly and distinctly, "the emergency is right here, sir."

A voice from behind Liffey said: "Come now, I'll carry you out Luv, if you're frightened." Liffey recognized the voice. It was the cute guard again! Where had *he* come from?

Feeling her credibility evaporating, Liffey tried to gather some presence of mind before she shredded her dignity once again and went on: "The *emergency* is right here with the Crowning Portrait. It's a fake! It's not real! It's a *copy* of the original! I have *proof.*"

There! Liffey had gotten everything out in less than ten seconds that she had been trying for the last hour to communicate to the gallery staff. Liffey scrambled for the poster which she had stuffed into her purse.

"There is an *extra pearl* in this portrait. If you would only *look* at the poster and then *look* at the portrait, you will see what I am talking about," Liffey begged as she thrust the poster into the hands of the handsome young gallery guard.

Liffey continued to explain: "There is an *extra pearl* on the queen's chain. Count from your left to your right. On the poster there is a gap. In the painting right in front of us, *there is no gap.* And the Winkie rhyme I used three years ago to count the pearls doesn't fit anymore either. Someone *switched* paintings. *Queen Elizabeth I's Crowning Portrait has been stolen!*"

"Oh no...." Out of the corner of her eye, Liffey detected a flash. Was there a photographer with the police and fire brigade? Was she going to be in the *paper*? Would they think *she* turned in the false alarm? That she was playing a prank? Was that a capital crime?

Her father would have *her* beheaded at the Tower of London, just like Henry VIII's wives. She could see the head of Liffey Rivers rolling around on Tower Green right now, with her father shaking his head sadly, possibly regretting his decision to execute his only child.

There was another flash. Then another flash. This was getting *serious* and Liffey felt flight hormones surging through her. The stupid siren was still screaming and Liffey wondered if anyone *ever* planned to turn it off. Only the cute guard's quizzical look kept her stationary.

"THIS YOUNG LADY IS CORRECT!!" he exclaimed. "There *is* an EXTRA PEARL on the Crowning Portrait. The painting on the wall is absolutely *not* identical to this poster!"

Liffey could have kissed him! He had come to her aid after all! She hoped he would get all the credit for calling attention to this problem. Maybe he would get a promotion or a medal, or a movie contract.

A television camera was aiming directly at Liffey and the cute guard. A TV reporter was looking into the camera saying, "This is Ann Strong, reporting live from the National Portrait Gallery, where we were called on a false fire alarm, but now we learn that a young American girl is claiming that the Crowning Portrait of Queen Elizabeth I hanging directly behind me, does not match up with the gallery's gift shop *poster* reproduction. She *insists* there is an extra pearl in the painting we are standing in front of now, and that she discovered this because the Wee Willie Winkie nursery rhyme did not *fit* the portrait at *this* gallery visit like it did when she was here three years ago."

Liffey heard some snickering in the crowd of policemen. She *wished* the reporter had not mentioned the Wee Willie Winkie rhyme on live television. It sounded very bizarre. It sounded crazy.

Liffey impulsively planted a little kiss on the cute guard's cheek, thanked him profusely and wished him luck solving the Crowning Portrait pearl mystery. Then she tried to blend into the large crowd which had gathered around the Crowning Portrait.

Liffey pulled the non-prescription, oversized glasses out of her purse and quickly put them on. She then tied her shoulder-length hair into a quick pony tail. Years of pony-tailing her hair quickly to put her Irish dance wigs on was paying off. She finished the disguise in seconds and headed towards the gallery stairs, praying that her father was not back in their B & B lounge watching the news.

She could probably get out of town without any more attention if she just remained cool and aloof. Nobody in London would have recognized her on camera. Just her dad.

If Liffey's luck would only hold, she would get on the plane for Ireland tomorrow morning and forget all about the Winkie pearl matter. She had an important feis coming up in just three more days, and tomorrow she would be picking up the most beautiful dress on earth in Dublin.

She had confidence that the cute guard would handle everything from now on.

CHAPTER TEN

Liffey was grateful that the Crowning Portrait was fairly close to the Tudor Gallery entrance, (or *exit*, if you were escaping from television cameras).

Liffey tried very hard to look lackadaisical, like she had not just been on television. Like she had not just said: "I am *positive* that the real painting has been replaced with a fake," on *television*, to England, and by now probably to the entire *universe*.

Escaping was going well so far. There did not seem to be any security guards or media people on the stairway. No doubt they were all inside the Tudor Gallery looking at the Crowning Portrait.

Liffey could see the main entrance now and picked up her pace. As she approached the front doors, her heart flip-flopped. There was a security screening station set up there with a monitor blocking the exit. In the monitor, Liffey could see her own enlarged face *freeze framed*. They were looking for her!

Liffey remembered that the jacket she was wearing was reversible. She quickly slipped out of it and reversed it to the jean jacket side instead of the geeky plaid side she had been wearing upstairs. She did look very different with the glasses and tied back hair. *How* different, would be determined if and when they let her out the front door. She would have to use a foreign accent because she had heard the camera woman *say* she was an American and she *had* opened her own big mouth and declared the portrait was a fake.

Liffey fervently hoped she would not panic again and start talking about fresh beet root in Portobello Road. She quickly thought of the idea to pretend she could not speak English.

"No hablos Ingles," would be her only hope. Liffey slowly approached the mobile security center and smiled shyly as she tried to walk blithely right through it. A sharp voice commanded her to stop. "Why you are still in this building young lady? It has been evacuated."

"Good," thought Liffey, "they don't recognize me!"

Liffey responded in her best junior high Spanish: "No comprendo. No hablo Ingles." Liffey hoped that her accent was convincing. The main security guard nodded and then, to Liffey's complete *horror*, starting conversing with her in fluent Spanish! *Real* Spanish! Not the junior high Senorita Nicolay Spanish Liffey used at school.

Senorita was an amazing teacher and Liffey was one of her best students, but this guy was babbling in Spanish so fast that Liffey could not even *pretend* to understand him. So she nodded a lot like she *did* understand what he was saying, and started to make her way to the front exit smiling and giving a little good-bye wave.

"I did it!" Liffey was ecstatic as the front door was opened for her by a security guard. "My disguise *worked*! Maybe I should be a spy when I grow up," Liffey daydreamed. "I can learn fifty languages and blend in anywhere. No one will know who I am, just like in Irish dancing. I will write only in Ogham and they will call me the 'taidhbhse.'" Liffey had taught herself a few Irish words when she had been studying Ogham symbols for her solo dress. The word 'taidhbhse,' which means 'ghost' in Irish, was one of her favorites, along with 'sidhe' which means 'fairy.'

Liffey practically flew across the Trafalgar Square plaza

and scrambled up the lion on her left. An adrenalin rush made her want to thump on her chest like Tarzan.

Liffey was so *thrilled* with her escape, that she did not see the three policemen to the left of the lion who were quietly waiting for her to descend.

***

Mr. Smith was having a late lunch in his favorite London pub. The steak and kidney pie here, he decided, was the best he'd ever had. As he sipped his mug of ale, he was distressed to see the publican turning on the pub's antique television.

Annoyed that the crackling TV was ruining the ambience he had come there for in the first place, he was startled to hear a familiar voice.

As the television finally came into focus, he could not believe what he was watching. It was that awful wig-girl again! *Now* she was in the National Portrait Gallery, trying to ruin his plans again! Somehow she *knew* that the Queen Elizabeth I Crowning Portrait was a fake.

Mr. Smith tried to keep his composure as he slowly stood up and exited the pub. "Not again," he moaned. "This *cannot* be happening again."

CHAPTER ELEVEN

Liffey remembered that it was almost time to meet her father in front of the National Portrait Gallery. He wanted to take her to lunch and then look into the matter of the 'misplaced' portrait of Princess Diana. He told Liffey that one of his clients was very suspicious and upset about the portrait's having been sent away for restoration purposes. How much 'restoration' could such a contemporary portrait need? Attorney Rivers wanted to verify with the gallery director that it had indeed gone missing by way of official channels. "In other words, Liffey, I intend to find out what's become of it."

Liffey was certain that her father would be very sympathetic to the fact that *she* had discovered the Queen Elizabeth I portrait was a fake, because he was so concerned about what had happened to the portrait of Princess Diana. He told Liffey that the Diana matter might be similar to a "whatever happened to the portraits of Queen Catherine Howard when Henry VIII wanted to pretend she had never existed?" situation. Liffey understood. It was the out-of-sight, out-of-mind rule.

Liffey slid down the lion's stony surface agilely and landed soundly on both feet, taking care to bend her knees slightly as she landed to lessen the impact. She began to make her way back to the National Portrait Gallery, oblivious to the fact that she was now being trailed by *six* policemen. She was anxious to tell her father about the Queen Elizabeth I portrait switch. He would know what to do. She had already alerted the gallery and it looked like the media was certainly on top of it, so Liffey assumed that her own role in the matter was over.

As Liffey walked towards the National Portrait Gallery, the six policemen were perplexed as to her gait. She seemed to be leaping forward sometimes and holding the leap in mid-air. Then she would do a skipping step and finally, what looked to be like scissors steps jumping up and down in place.

The officers wondered why they were following an obviously little girl who seemed to be more intent upon flapping her feet than anything else. Their instructions, however, were quite clear. Fan out and do *not* let her out of their sight.

Liffey was in front of the art gallery now, relieved that she had evaded detection. As she blended in with the large crowd which had gathered outside, she felt clever and secretly delighted that she had slipped through the police net inside the gallery.

She did *not* want her father to find out she had been the center of attention again inside the gallery. She had promised him that she would be on perfect behavior, which of course, she *had* been. All she had done was to alert the British government that one of their national treasures was missing. That was *hardly* misbehaving.

Liffey considered the possibility that she might have even received an important medal for her detective work except for the fact that she had not told anyone her name and she wanted the cute guard to get the credit.

"Perfect timing," Liffey thought as she observed her father alighting from a taxi cab. She ran up to him and gave him one of her biggest hugs. "Whoa!" he exclaimed. "What have I done to deserve such a welcome?"

"Excuse me, sir," a voice directly behind him said. "I regret to inform you that you must come with us for questioning."

Before Liffey could even clue her father in as to the events that had transpired not even thirty minutes ago, he was hustled into a police van over his loud objections.

There were suddenly a million cameras flashing and another television lady reporting: "It seems that Scotland Yard has already taken a suspect into custody for questioning." Cameras started flashing again as Liffey felt herself being hoisted into the police van beside her father.

The police van was surrounded by frantic press who were desperately trying to get more photos and video of Liffey and her father.

Robert Rivers, trying to make the best of the incredible confusion going on around him, calmly looked at his daughter and simply said: "Say Liff, would you like to fill me in here?"

Liffey could not believe what was happening! She did not even know where to begin. *How* could her detecting a fraudulent portrait in the National Portrait Gallery have gotten herself, and now her father, into so much hot water?

"Well, Daddy, you know how you are always saying that no good deed ever goes unpunished?"

"Yes," Robert Rivers replied.

"Well, *my* good deed is being punished!"

"And just what *is* the good deed you performed here in London, today, Liff?" Mr. Rivers bottom lip was trembling, but he managed not to raise his voice.

"I discovered that the Crowning Portrait of Queen Elizabeth I was a *fake*," Liffey explained excitedly.

"I see," said her father. Liffey noted that he was now biting his bottom lip.

"And just *how* did you figure *that* out and *why* are we now headed to Scotland Yard to explain ourselves?"

Liffey could tell her father was about to erupt, so she

hurriedly went on: "Well, there was this poor, totally *pathetic* old lady hauling around a bunch of little brats in the Tudor Gallery and she was losing it, so I tried to take over for her and started to explain to the little monsters that there was a *fake* portrait of Queen Elizabeth I in the Gallery and I would show them how I found out using the Wee Willie Winkie rhyme. Then, I think I told them that it was an emergency. The next thing I knew, there were sirens going off and everybody shouting and leaving the building.

I stayed behind though to explain to the security guards about number 44, the extra pearl, and the cute guard believed me because I showed him the gift shop poster of the real Crowning Portrait and it clearly did *not* have the extra pearl, so the Winkie rhyme was right.

Then, I left because I wanted the cute guard that I had so *pathetically* asked about fresh beet root in Portobello Road to get all the credit for the switched portrait. I put on a disguise and slipped out of the building so I could practice for the feis while I was waiting for you. But I climbed a lion instead and *then* when I got down to find you…well *you know* what happened *then*, because here we are!"

"Yes, *here we are*," Robert Rivers sighed without expression. Liffey observed her father taking out his mobile phone, scrolling down the menu and then pressing a key. She put her iPod headphones back into her ears, deciding she did *not* want to hear what her father was saying to whoever it was he had called. It *had* to be bad. She would listen to that song about being over the rainbow instead.

CHAPTER TWELVE

The police van pulled slowly away from the curb and threaded its way through the huge traffic jam. At least they did not turn on the siren.

Liffey could see that there were soldiers now among the spectators. She thought she heard a helicopter but was too weary to look. "Yet *another* Liffey Rivers Reality Show," she thought miserably.

Liffey could feel big tears beginning to flow down her face. Robert Rivers put his left arm around Liffey's slight shoulders. Liffey glanced at him and saw that he was beginning to laugh again, just like he had done three years ago after the nanny dodging incident. She hoped he had not entirely flipped out like the poor docent. Liffey could not see *any* humor in this possible arrest situation that she had dragged her father into.

After the police car had traveled several long blocks, it suddenly did a U-turn and quickly headed back in the opposite direction. Robert Rivers did not seem to be perturbed by this, but Liffey was.

Were they heading *back* to where the whole catastrophe began? If her father would only *stop* laughing, Liffey would ask him what was so funny. He was starting to freak her out.

This was a nightmare. Liffey could see Trafalgar Square again and it was mobbed with television crews and fire trucks and police riot squad officers and reporters of all shapes and sizes. And nosy people. There must have been a thousand nosy people. Why was the police car *returning* them to this madness?

Maybe she was going to be *beheaded* on The National Portrait Gallery steps as an example of what happens if sirens go off by mistake and the whole firefighting brigade of London turns up.

Liffey of course was innocent, but look what had happened to Anne Boleyn and Catherine Howard!

Surely, she would at *least* get a trial? She also needed to get competent medical help for her poor father. She had finally driven him over the edge of the biggest cliff yet. He simply could no longer cope with Liffey and all the trouble she was always getting into. She did not blame him. She wondered if his odd sister, her Aunt Jean, might actually be helpful in finding a nice, quiet place for him to go to while he recovered his sanity. If he ever *did* recover it. Liffey feared she may have permanently robbed him of any future mental health as she listened to him snorting with laughter.

The 'Rivers Show' pulled up along the side of the National Portrait Gallery. One of their police escort jumped out of the van and opened the back door for Liffey and her father.

They were getting out *here*? Maybe she really *was* about to be beheaded! The policeman who opened the van door for them stood back respectfully while Liffey awkwardly clamored out. It was a long drop down to the pavement. At least she was fairly certain that there had not been time to call in a French swordsman. Anne Boleyn had *asked* Henry VIII to get the French swordsman. Liffey thought she herself would prefer the ax method.

Behind her, Liffey could hear her father chuckling as he descended much more efficiently than Liffey.

"Daddy," Liffey whispered, "you have to STOP *laughing.*

This is serious! I think we're in a lot of trouble and I see television cameras everywhere. You don't want to be seen on TV making fun of all this. It could get worse, you know."

Before Mr. Rivers had time to reassure his daughter, a humongous grey limousine pulled up next to the police van blocking a whole lane of traffic.

The chauffeur jumped out and opened the door for a handsome, important-looking middle-aged man, who was wearing an incredible blue pinstriped suit and a big smile. This guy could *not* be the executioner. And if he *was*, his cheerful demeanor "is in really poor taste," thought Liffey. She wondered if everybody was standing around grinning right before Anne Boleyn's head went flying.

Now there were so many cameras flashing that the grey London day had become absolutely radiant. This guy had bodyguards too, Liffey observed, wondering who on *earth* he could be.

Maybe she was dreaming. This whole thing *had* become very surrealistic and weird. Even for a Liffey Rivers' day. If she could only just wake up, she could go to the National Portrait Gallery and look at the Queen Elizabeth I portraits and not have all this extra drama attached to it.

She needed to be practicing for the feis in Ireland. She did *not* need to be a guest of Scotland Yard and now apparently this celebrity as well.

To make this whole scene seem *completely* from outer space, Liffey's father *walked right up* to the pinstriped man, like he actually *knew* him, pulling her along with him.

"Liffey, I would like you to meet the Prime Minister," Robert Rivers said warmly, shaking hands with this minister like he *knew* this prime minister. Like they played golf together or something. What did 'prime' mean anyway? Probably *first* or *best* minister, like a 'prime' rib. The only prime minister Liffey could think of was Winston Churchill and she was fairly certain he was dead.

"It's an honor to meet you, Liffey. It seems you have had quite a day and that Great Britain is truly *indebted* to you for your questioning the *authenticity* of our Queen Elizabeth I Crowning Portrait." He flashed his game show host smile at Liffey.

Liffey almost asked him if he knew that you could get fresh beet root in Portobello Road.

Instead, she answered politely, like she was in a movie, "It is an honor for me as well, sir." She wanted to add "Can we *pleeeease* get out of here now?"

Liffey was surprised to see that her father seemed to be on a first name basis with this man. Liffey suddenly realized that there must be an awful lot she did not know about her father. Maybe she would have to stop talking so much about Irish dance with him and ask him a few questions about himself once in awhile.

Immediately following their last-minute reprieve by the Prime Minister, Liffey and her father were put into another limo which was obviously waiting for *them* and whisked away again.

"Well, Liffey, it seems you have done it again," her father said warmly as they drove off to "who knows where this time," Liffey thought crossly.

"You know, Liffey," Robert Rivers said, "that Sherlock Holmes and you are beginning to have a lot in common. Both of you notice the little things that most people just walk right by. You are both very high strung and each of you has amazing intuition."

"Yeah, I guess so," Liffey replied, thinking the only

really, really important thing on her mind at the moment was getting to Dublin tomorrow and getting that solo dress. And practicing her steps. She knew if she were to place at the Beltra Feis, she was going to have to get some *serious* practicing in. And with all this Queen Elizabeth I portrait stuff to wade through, she was beginning to fear she would not have enough time or energy to work on her dancing.

Especially the dreaded Hornpipe. Liffey wished she could get some divine intervention with her Hornpipe. Or that it might be *eliminated* from competitions entirely because it was so *annoying*.

If the feis were going to be in England, Liffey thought, she could ask the Prime Minister to get the Hornpipe *removed* from the schedule as a really good way to show how grateful he was to her for exposing the fake Queen Elizabeth I portrait.

CHAPTER THIRTEEN

New Scotland Yard was very disappointing. It was nothing like the one described in the Sherlock Holmes stories Liffey had read with mist swirling around and Bobbies patrolling with their night sticks and mysterious shadows everywhere. Liffey's father said that was because the Old Scotland Yard was long gone and this new block long, twenty-stories-high building was built because London was now a city of a zillion people.

"Liffey," Robert Rivers began, "when we get in there, you *must* follow my lead. I know how you figured out that the portrait had been switched using your nursery rhyme counting method, but I am your father and I know how you think. The police are probably consulting a child psychologist at this very moment to find out what deep meaning this Wee Willie Winkie rhyme has and why you needed to express yourself in a rhyme instead of regular talk. That kind of nonsense."

Liffey giggled as Robert Rivers continued, "and make no mistake, this so-called *voluntary* statement thing we are here to do is not really voluntary, is it? I don't remember *either* of us asking anyone if we could come here and talk about things. They are bringing us in to try to determine if you know more than you are letting on. The reason they grabbed me, is because before I called my staff in Chicago and told them that we needed help, the police assumed that I was involved in the portrait theft and that you were a chatty little kid who wanted to tell the world about it. So watch my face for cues. I will interrupt and not allow you to answer any questions which might be designed to trap you or confuse you. The police are only doing their job. They have to launch a huge investigation now, and you, my dear, are the beginning of it!"

"But the Prime Minister *congratulated* me, Daddy. He even shook my hand. Why are the police acting like I did something wrong?"

"It's the 'no-good-deed-ever-goes-unpunished' rule again, Liffey. I swear that seems to be the way the world works. If it gets rough in there, I will turn on the mean-lawyer part of my brain, as you would put it, and we will walk right out. For now though, the police really do need you to tell them as much as you can.

You can start by teaching them the Wee Willie Winkie rhyme if you like!"

***

Mr. Smith paced the floor of his tiny hotel room. He needed to have an *authentic* Irish name for the feis but he couldn't think of one. He wanted a little mystery and charm attached to the name as well. Nothing came to mind. *Finally* a name came to him. He would be 'Donald McFleury,' adjudicator *par excellence*. The name 'McFleury' seemed somewhat familiar and he thought it suited him. He would have to use an English accent, however, because he could not master a believable Irish brogue in twenty-four hours.

He was to meet with the carrier at 4:00 p.m. this afternoon to make the final arrangements and then head out to the Holyhead ferry by train. His custom-made stage would accompany him to the feis because he insisted that when *he* was the adjudicator, his dancers would only dance on the very best wood and the sturdiest stage platform. None of Adjudicator McFleury's dancers were going to slip and fall, because he cared so *deeply* about their welfare.

He looked into the small wall mirror and practiced winking. He wanted to appear to be friendly and kind and thought that winking at the dancers would be a nice touch.

It would show them that he was not a robot like most of the other judges he had observed at feiseanna.

CHAPTER FOURTEEN

Liffey and her father were escorted into a little conference room and given cups of tea. Liffey decided to use this down-time to do some much needed pre-feis stretching, so she sat on the floor and assumed the yoga position, breathing deeply in and out and out and in.

When she felt centered, she un-tucked her legs and extended them out and into a V. Then she began the all-important stretching. She did *not* want to fall at the feis in Ireland. She wanted to be as limber as possible.

Liffey did not hear the door open because she had her iPod playing her practice Slip Jig music. A hawk-nosed man in a Mr. Rogers kind of cardigan had walked in, trying to act casual. Liffey could tell from her stretching position on the floor that he seemed ill at ease. Probably because her father was an internationally acclaimed lawyer and Attorney Rivers was sitting in the interrogation room with her as both father *and* lawyer.

Liffey fully intended to cooperate so she and her dad could get *out* as quickly as possible. No hissing or growling today.

She jumped up from the floor and gave the too thin, nervous child psychologist, her best Little Orphan Annie smile. Liffey was absolutely *beaming* at him when she caught the "watch it, Liffey!" look from her father.

She toned herself down immediately and said: "Good afternoon, sir. I suppose you are here to talk with me?" The skinny man looked relieved and answered, "as a matter of fact, young lady, I am."

***

A few hours later, on their two mile walk back to The Ridgemount Hotel, following an *enormous* shrimp fried rice dinner in Chinatown, Robert Rivers congratulated his daughter on the way she had conducted herself during the interview with the child psychologist, and later with the Chief Inspector in the fraud division of Scotland Yard. "I only had to interject lawyer talk twice, Liffey. You were a pro."

"Well, Daddy, how many shrink and legal questions can anyone be asked about Wee Willie Winkie?" Liffey quipped as she launched into her Reel, distancing herself from her father.

***

Robert Rivers barely noticed the olive-skinned, stylishly dressed woman directly across the wide avenue from him. She was window shopping with her cute little poodle dog, chattering away at it like the dog could understand everything she said.

CHAPTER FIFTEEN

The woman and the poodle walked quickly past The Ridgemount Hotel B & B. Then she crossed the street and headed towards the Royal Academy of Dramatic Art where she handed the little dog to a young man on a motorcycle. He sped off with the miniature poodle tucked into a deep side basket and the woman turned around and walked back to The Ridgemount. She opened the door of a green van parked across the street and climbed inside, noting with pleasure the large steaming mug of coffee with her name on it.

***

Mr. McFleury decided that he could not bear the thought of another long train ride, so he rented a car to drive to the Holyhead Ferry. Besides, he needed to get from Dublin to Sligo when he arrived in Ireland, and he was determined to follow his stage from the docks to the feis. He had worked so hard on it and could not bear the thought of some careless driver bouncing it around on back roads. He would follow the stage and make sure it arrived in perfect condition. The wellbeing of his dancers meant *everything* to him. So did the stage.

***

Robert Rivers gazed at Liffey sleeping soundly in the bed across the room, clutching Mrs. Pooh, her stuffed monkey.

She looked so *little*. How could she keep walking into such *big* conspiracies? And then, somehow manage to unravel them? Was she psychic? Gifted? Destined for glory? He feared that one day she might actually leap into deep waters, way over her head. He must see to it that she never drowned. How he longed for her mother, Maeve, and her innate ability to always know what was best for Liffey. Maeve would have known what to do about the screaming dreams. All he could do was wait for them to start and then try to reassure Liffey that she was safe.

CHAPTER SIXTEEN

Liffey was startled awake and looked at her alarm clock. It was 6:00 a.m. already. She leapt out of bed and tried not to wake her father up as she did a jig step in place. Today was **THE** day. It was the most important day of her life to date. It was **SOLO DRESS DAY!** She grabbed Mrs. Pooh and did a wild polka around the room.

Their plane for Dublin left at noon and they needed to catch the train from Liverpool Station to Stansted Airport no later than 8:00 a.m. They would eat a good breakfast downstairs in the pleasant dining room, grab a cab and leave London at last!

No more "whatever happened to Queen Elizabeth I's Crowning Portrait?" questions. Liffey wished she had *never* started the whole thing in the first place. At least the press had no clue what had become of Liffey and her father.

They had been taken out of New Scotland Yard through a secret tunnel and put into an unmarked patrol car which dropped them off at Leicester Square as they requested.

The limo they had arrived in at police headquarters left with decoys for the Savoy Hotel with the entire London media army in pursuit. They would never think to look for the wealthy Rivers family at a moderately priced B & B in Bloomsbury.

***

The attractive poodle woman sitting in the green van had

finished three cups of coffee by the time dawn finally came with its chorus of song birds. "If you're not up at dawn in London, you miss the birds," she thought dreamily. The night had been long and predictably boring. She fervently hoped she was not going to have to spend the next six hours of her shift sitting in this van across from the B & B trying to stay awake.

At approximately 7:15 a.m., a taxicab pulled up in front of The Ridgemount. The poodle woman anxiously focused on the front door which was opening almost simultaneously. The man and his daughter emerged carrying suitcases, confirming that they were leaving the premises. "Time to go," she thought gratefully as she turned on the ignition.

***

The train from Liverpool Station was on time. Liffey and her father sleepily claimed seats with a table so Robert Rivers could write on his laptop. Liffey wanted to sleep some more and sprawled out. They were *finally* headed to Dublin! Liffey had become philosophical about her long solo dress waiting ordeal. She understood now how the Pilgrims must have felt when they landed on Plymouth Rock (except Liffey thought she remembered reading that they had *not* actually landed there). At any rate, she had traveled for a long, *long* time on this journey for her first solo dress and within a few hours, she would be trying it on. If only she were not still so sleepy, she could do some ankle flexing and toe pointing….

Robert Rivers pretended not to see the poodle woman who was sitting ten seating sections away from them on the opposite side of the train. He was fairly certain that he had seen her before and recently, but could not remember where. She looked friendly enough, and he did not have any sense of foreboding as he watched her paging through a magazine. At

64

the moment at hand, he had reports to write and a million other things on which to concentrate. He would think about her later if he saw her again. Three times and it would *not* be a coincidence. He admired her layered auburn hair which clashed somewhat with her creamy olive complexion. He filed her in his 'visual memory box' and continued his letter to the National Portrait Gallery, explaining why he had missed his appointment concerning the Princess Diana portrait.

Liffey slept on the train the entire way to the airport. She liked all this traveling around like real people without a limousine that she and her father had been doing since they had arrived in London. There had been open air double-decker bus rides, underground tube rides, and best of all, the black taxicabs. Her father *loved* riding around in those.

He told Liffey that there had been cabs in London since 1639. "Of course," he pointed out to her, "the *early* cabs had been horse-drawn." Liffey resisted a "You're kidding, right?" retort. Like she would *really* think there would have been automobiles in 1639!

Sometimes she thought her father treated her like a two-year-old, but Robert Rivers *acted* like *he* was a two-year-old whenever he had a cooperative London cabbie driving them around. He knew that London cabs were designed to turn in tight circles, and asked the drivers if they would mind demonstrating these tricky maneuvers over and over again. Liffey thought it was *totally* embarrassing. It was like being out on the town with a little *brother*, not a father. Liffey was happy that this train connected with the airport so she and her father would not have to hire another cab.

***

Mr. McFleury was having second thoughts about the

ferry boat ride to Dublin as he drove north towards Wales. He thought that ferry boat rides were as bad, and possibly worse, than riding the train. Too public and far too many noisy children. He could not understand why their parents did not seem to be able to control them. They ran all over the boat like packs of wild dogs. Only dogs made less noise. He hoped that the dancers at the Beltra Feis would not be squealing and laughing.

Children depressed Mr. McFleury. He tried to keep in character and remain focused on his objective. The safe stage and how *kind* and *thoughtful* he was to provide his dancers with such luxury. The day after tomorrow his 'safe stage' would be headed for its final resting place. The bottom of the Atlantic Ocean.

***

The shift change at Stansted Airport did not happen. The poodle woman realized that her replacement would not arrive until fifteen minutes *after* the final boarding time which the airline rigidly enforced. Sometimes sleep was not an option in her life. Today was one of those days. She could get an hour in on the plane maybe. But she needed more if she was to tail the Rivers family efficiently. With a deep sigh, she realized she would be drinking a lot of coffee in Dublin. Maybe she would switch to tea.

CHAPTER SEVENTEEN

L iffey and her father left the busy Dublin airport to catch a shuttle van to claim their rental car. A million thoughts raced across her brain like she was channel surfing.

Would the dress *fit*?

What if she *hated* it?

How could she *hate* it-she had *designed* it!

What if the *material* was not quite right?

What if the Ogham alphabet was *wrong*?

What if the unusual blue color tones looked *terrible* on her?

What if it made her look *fat*?

What if it made her look too *thin*?

What if the dressmaker was not *ready* for her today?

Liffey was fully aware of what a pest she had been with the poor seamstress and her staff. "I was even worse than some of the worst diva mothers," she thought regretfully.

She had vowed to herself that she would *never* be completely demanding and desperate waiting for her solo dress. But she feared she *had been* very, very demanding.

It occurred to Liffey that solo dress quests seemed to bring out the best and the worst in everyone.

***

Don Dailey's rental car was *Japanese*. Liffey was disappointed. She had expected cars in Ireland to be *Irish*.

As they approached the city center, Liffey was surprised to note that here as in England, everybody was driving on the *wrong* side of the road again.

"Why do they drive on the left *here*, don't they like Napoleon either?" Her father had told Liffey in London that the British made driving on the *left* the legal side of the road because their arch-enemy Napoleon had made driving on the *right* side of the road the legal side. She was getting car sick from this left side of the road thing.

There was a pause in the conversation and Liffey quickly realized her mistake, but it was too late. Her father glowed as he began what was going to be *another* one of his history lectures and Liffey had brought this one upon herself with the *stupid* Napoleon question!

Robert Rivers began his discourse: "In 1798, Irish revolutionaries led by Wolfe Tone were trying to persuade revolutionary France to come and help them drive the English out of Ireland. Napoleon, however, thought conquering Egypt was a better idea. So he took his army there. The Irish rebels were very disappointed, and they lost once again. So they probably didn't like Napoleon much either. Napoleon finally lost too. After he was exiled to the island of St. Helena, Napoleon said his decision not to help the Irish was the worst mistake he ever made."

"Daddy, think I have to throw up."

***

Although it looked like a very large city, at least as big as Milwaukee, there did not seem to be any really tall buildings in Dublin. The tallest things around looked like old churches, and domes and towers with statues. She was tempted to ask her father if he knew why but didn't dare risk another history lesson.

Liffey begged her father to drive directly to the solo dress shop before they did any sight-seeing.

Robert Rivers immediately agreed that it was a *great* idea to get the dress first, but informed Liffey that they would have to go back a bit to Glasnevin. This seemed to make him *very* happy and Liffey was concerned that there might be another reason why her father was anxious to get to the Glasnevin place.

He handed Liffey a map and told her to find Finglas Road. "It's just to the north of the Royal Canal."

***

As Liffey got out of the car into the neighborhood where dreams come true, she noticed a tall, skinny white tower that came to a point on top across the street in a huge cemetery. It looked like the Washington Monument but it was round instead of square. Liffey was afraid to ask her father what it was because she could see the glint in his eyes.

He *knew* that tower was there all the time. *That* was why he had seemed happy to go for the dress *before* they drove through Dublin City.

He was a spider sitting in his web waiting for Liffey, the fly, to get stuck. Liffey knew he was waiting for her to ask him what the tower was, but she was not going to fall into that trap. She had been caught in her history nut father's web too many times. Liffey often thought her father should have been a history professor instead of an attorney.

All Liffey wanted to see in Dublin was the River Liffey, which she was named after, the statue of poor Molly Malone who died with a fever and the Book of Kells at Trinity College.

And she wanted to 'shake hands' with the 900-year-old crusader who was now a *mummy* in the basement crypt of St. Michan's Church.

She feared her father would want to see a zillion other things. It would probably take him five years or more to tour Dublin the way he would like to and there was only the rest of today and tomorrow until early afternoon. Then they would be off to County Sligo to get a good rest before the Beltra Feis the following day.

***

With her precious solo dress safely deposited in the solo dress carrier, Liffey Rivers wondered if it were possible to be happier than she was at this moment. She doubted it.

The dress was a *perfect* fit and the metallic, watery blues suited her fair complexion. The new wig, with the solo dress crown and sparkling tiara carefully centered, made Liffey think that fairy tales do come true. At least her 'Solo Dress Quest' one did.

The simplicity of her dress design had impressed the seamstress who was much more accustomed to assembling multi-colored, complicated dresses. "Your dress is very dignified," she told Liffey. "Using the Ogham alphabet (Liffey did not tell the kind lady, but she had not slanted some of the Ogham marks quite enough to the right) was a stroke of genius." Liffey liked the word genius. No one had ever used that word before when they were referring to Liffey Rivers. Certainly not the teachers at her middle school in Wisconsin.

***

Liffey was in such ecstasy holding her solo dress carrier which was *finally occupied*, that she cheerfully asked her father now about the monument across the street.

Now she was ready for the Robert Rivers Dublin lecture series. She was ready for anything! He began it by explaining to Liffey that a zillion Irish patriots were buried in the Glasnevin Cemetery right across the street!

People like Charles Parnell, Michael Collins, Constance Markievicz, Roger Casement and Patrick Pearse. He explained that the big white round tower was where Daniel O'Connell, who was called the Liberator or something, was laid to rest. As she walked through the cemetery with Robert Rivers, she was grateful she had a father who had made all of this happiness possible. "Today belongs to Daddy," Liffey smiled. He deserved to have an audience to share with them his extensive knowledge of Irish history. Liffey could spend tonight and tomorrow mentally and physically preparing herself for the Beltra Feis. She hoped they had spaghetti in Sligo for the pre-feis ritual dinner. She had forgotten to pack spaghetti noodles for a possible 'no spaghetti available' emergency. She also needed to get bagels and turkey and cheese and tomatoes for the pre-feis ritual breakfast.

CHAPTER EIGHTEEN

L iffey," began Robert Rivers, "I realize how anxious you are to see the statue of Molly Malone, but I must tell you that she may have never even existed."

After that bombshell, he applied orange marmalade to his toast.

Molly Malone was the first song Liffey had taught herself to play on her tin whistle. She usually cried and had to stop playing when she got to the "She died of a fever, and no one could save her, and that was the end of sweet Molly Malone; but her ghost wheels her barrow, through streets broad and narrow, crying 'cockles and mussels alive, alive oh!'" part of the ballad.

Her father continued to ruin Liffey's day. "You see the song is technically not even named Molly Malone. It was written by a Scotsman and he called it 'Cockles and Mussels,' I think."

"Whatever," replied Liffey pretending not to care. But Liffey *did* care. Many times Liffey had imagined poor Molly Malone, all feverish and barely alive, struggling to push her wheel barrow full of cockles and mussels through the crowded Dublin streets.

"What's next?" Liffey muttered. She answered her own question, "*next* is my father telling me there really was no Rose and Jack on the Titanic." Liffey determined right then and there before she devoured her huge Irish breakfast she would *never, ever* discuss the Titanic disaster with her father. She would have to be careful since she knew the ship was built in Ireland up in Belfast.

Liffey was fairly certain that all her father's obsessing with what *was* real and what was *not* real, stemmed from an experience in his own life.

Robert Rivers' *real* first name was Christopher. Shortly after Christopher Robert Rivers was born, there was a big stink about Saint Christopher, the saint he was named after, never having existed.

Liffey had heard from her Aunt Jean that this declaration that there had never been such a saint had upset her grandmother, big time, because she had named her only son after her favorite saint, and suddenly the saint was history.

Or technically, *not* history.

Poof! He was just gone. Blotted out like disappearing magic ink that vanishes after you put it on a piece of paper and wait thirty seconds. So her grandmother had called her father 'Robert' from then on and kind of forgot about the 'Christopher' part of her baby boy's name.

Liffey, however, decided that Molly Malone *was* real, no matter *what* her lawyer father, *Christopher* Robert Rivers, had to say about her. This poor feverish lady was totally *real*, and she, Liffey Rivers, would walk some narrow Dublin streets later on today and see if Molly's ghost flickered by wheeling a wheel barrow.

***

It seemed to Liffey that she and her father had left London weeks ago, but it actually had been less than twenty-four hours since they had flown over the Irish Sea and seen the tiny ferry boat skimming over the water far below them. It looked like a boat that was water skiing. Robert Rivers told his daughter it was a fast hovercraft ferry and was able to get all the way from Holyhead in Wales to Dublin in about two hours.

***

At the same moment, Mr. McFleury was on the deck of the Holyhead-Dublin ferry boat, idly watching the airplane above, and trying not to think about his stage in the boat's container area below sea level. It was a calm day so it was unlikely that any water would be seeping into the cargo hold. Even if it did, his stage had been wrapped in layers and layers of heavy plastic and then professionally sealed. In forty-eight hours the stage would be going to Davy Jones' locker but by then it would have served its purpose. No dancers would have been injured doing their steps on *this* adjudicator's stage.

***

Liffey carefully studied the statue of Molly Malone at the end of Grafton Street. She was glad Molly had a statue. Why should Queen Elizabeth I have all those portraits and *real* women like Molly Malone have no memorials to commemorate their lives?

It was while Robert Rivers was positioning Liffey for a photo between Molly Malone and her wheelbarrow that he caught a glimpse of an olive-skinned, auburn haired woman who was also photographing Molly Malone from a distance.

This was the third time.

CHAPTER NINETEEN

Liffey was relieved to hear her father's proclamation. "Got it, Liff!"

Robert Rivers continued to smile at Liffey as if he had *not* seen someone who was obviously following them.

Who *was* she and was she dangerous? Did she think Liffey *knew* where the missing portrait of Queen Elizabeth I was? Did she think *he* was involved?

***

After Liffey's terrifying ordeal in St. Louis earlier in the summer, Robert Rivers was still trying to convince Liffey that she was safe and that the screaming dreams would end. He decided *not* to tell Liffey that they were now being followed. He *did* tell Liffey that they would leave Dublin right after they did a quick look see of the Book of Kells at Trinity College.

Liffey had been disappointed after breakfast that they had not been able to see the crusader's mummy at St. Michan's. There had been some kind of restoration crew there and the underground crypts had not been open to the public.

The other 'must see and do in Dublin' places on Liffey's list had been a great success. They had walked across the Ha'Penny Bridge arched over her namesake, the River Liffey. She had found the bullet holes in the Daniel O'Connell statue in front of the famous bridge across the Liffey that was wider than it was long. She had admired the statues in the general

Post Office where the 1916 Rising had begun. They had tea and lunch at Bewley's and watched the street performers on Grafton Street. They had even managed to go through the National History Museum and see the *real* Tara Brooch, the St. Patrick's Tooth shrine from County Sligo and amazing Celtic gold jewelry.

Liffey decided that the National Art Gallery in Dublin was easier to do than the one in England, and fell in love with an oil painting called 'The Wounded Poacher.' The poor poacher had been shot for stealing two rabbits that lay dead at his feet in the painting. "At least he got away with the rabbits," thought Liffey.

Robert Rivers knew how anxious Liffey was to get to County Sligo and start her peculiar pre-feis rituals. He also knew that if he began to lecture her about the Vikings who had settled here in Dublin and the Norman conquests and the turbulent history of the 1916 Rising, Liffey would panic and *beg to get out* of Dublin. He would not have to frighten her by telling her they *had* to leave Dublin because he was determined to elude the stylish stalker.

***

"*Enough already!*" Liffey shrieked. For some unknown reason, her father had launched into a non-stop, not even coming up for air lecture like Liffey was in some kind of Irish studies *graduate* degree program at some university or something. He had been babbling now for thirty minutes about Vikings and some guy named Strongbow and Dublin Castle.

"Daddy, you know how much *I love* all this history stuff and everything, but we really better be on our way to Sligo *soon* because I *have* to practice for the feis tomorrow."

To Liffey's relief and amazement, her father *agreed* that they had better be on their way. As they walked along, he continued to ramble on about Irish patriots and cruel deaths, but Liffey noticed that he looked mechanical and that he seemed to be preoccupied about something.

Then he did something so bizarre that Liffey did not know *what* to make of it. He hailed a taxi when they were only about two blocks away from the place they had parked their rental car!

Surely he did not think that these regular looking car cabs could do the tight turns he had been so obsessed with in London in the black taxi cabs?

Then he behaved even *more* peculiarly. After Liffey pointed out that they had *passed* the side street where they had parked the rental car, he asked the cab driver to take them to the *bus* station!

As Liffey protested, he told her he was comparing *Dublin* cabs with *London* cabs as to road worthiness and to please just humor him. It would only take a few minutes.

"Are you thinking about becoming a cab driver, Daddy?" Liffey asked sarcastically. She knew her father could be strange sometimes but he was beginning to act like a lunatic.

The instant he paid their cab driver at the bus station, Robert Rivers grabbed Liffey's hand and pulled her *into* the bus station and through the back door of the terminal where the busses were loading people and across the street into yet *another* taxi cab!

"Why can't we just ride the same cab we *came in back* to our car?" Liffey demanded.

"Because, I need to *test* another cab, Liffey. I can't make my comparison after only having ridden in *one* Dublin cab, can I?" he asked, like he was *not* totally demented.

Liffey was speechless. They rode in silence back to their

rental car. Liffey hoped her father was not going to become a taxi cab historian or something and spend the rest of his life testing cabs everywhere. "The stress of being a lawyer had finally taken him out," thought Liffey sadly.

***

The poodle woman was obviously distressed and frustrated. Robert Rivers and his daughter, Liffey, had *vanished*. She had *lost* them. She would have to call for back up help here in Dublin and display her incompetence to everyone. At least she had the license plate and general description of their rental car. Reluctantly, she called her Dublin contact and admitted defeat.

"Olivia, my dear, don't fret! We'll get right back to you when we pick up their trail," the efficient voice comforted with what sounded like an Irish-German accent.

CHAPTER TWENTY

Robert Rivers was driving his red Toyota just under the speed limit on the Longford Road. He had always thought that the drivers on the Autobahn in Germany were speed maniacs, but these Irish drivers were passing him on this dual carriageway like he was standing still. "These idiots must be driving at the speed of light. What's the big rush? *I'm* the one being followed and I'm driving at the speed limit," he thought irritably.

Liffey's immediate concern was lining up the pre-feis spaghetti dinner. She would *totally* jinx the feis tomorrow if she did not eat spaghetti and meatballs tonight. How *could* she have forgotten to pack the spaghetti noodles? They wouldn't have taken up much room in her suitcase and then she would not be worrying right now about whether or not she would be able to find spaghetti in Sligo tonight.

Robert Rivers could not *believe* Liffey was doing the spaghetti routine again. After all the excitement in London, she was *still completely* preoccupied with not 'jinxing' her feis. He assured her that finding a spaghetti dinner in Sligo was going to be easy.

***

Mr. McFleury watched the container marked 'Beltra Feis, Sligo' being loaded on to the waiting lorry. Customs was a non-issue and he was on the road in no time behind the truck headed to County Sligo.

***

Olivia's Dublin contact had tracked the Rivers' rental car to the Longford Road heading northwest. Since she was only a block from Connolly Station, she was told to take the Sligo train heading northwest which was leaving in ten minutes. She was to get off the train at Longford where a 2007 green Picasso would be waiting for her. The keys would be in the glove compartment. "Only in Ireland," Olivia smiled, "would the keys to a brand new car be deposited in the *glove compartment* of a thief-magnet car." She was to receive further instructions in Longford, and was politely told not to lose the Rivers family again.

***

The driving was getting better. Ireland was starting to look pretty amazing to Liffey. The rolling midlands were morphing into spectacular mountains. She felt a little rush of adrenaline when she realized she was *part* of all this majesty because most of her mother's ancestors were from the northwest of Ireland. It made her want to ask her father to stop the car so she could get out and hug everybody. After all, they *could* be related to her!

There was *still* the matter of the spaghetti and meatballs dinner to worry about because Liffey knew her father did not take the jinxing seriously. He might try to take her out to dinner in a castle or something where they would not even know what spaghetti was.

As they drove into County Sligo, Liffey could see that on top of many of the mountains there were what appeared to be little piles of rocks, like toppings on a sundae. Robert Rivers told her that they were called 'cairns' and that these were ancient burial places. Liffey thought it would be amazing to be buried on the very top of a mountain and happily remembered that she and her father were planning to climb Knocknarea after the feis tomorrow to visit Queen Maeve's pile of rocks tomb.

***

Mr. McFleury was utterly beside himself. He was standing in front of a small, dark, red-sided building that looked like an American barn, watching the lorry pull away. *This* was *Beltra Hall?* It had never occurred to him that the Beltra Feis would be in the middle of *nowhere* and that there would be no activity there the day before the big feis. His beloved stage was safe in its ocean container in the small parking lot, but he needed to get it inside and in place. He couldn't just leave it here outside. Fortunately, he did have a contact number for a Mrs. O'Connor. He hoped she would be able to come and round up a few strong Irish farmers to help him set up. Otherwise, he might have to spend the night sleeping in his car to make sure nothing happened to his stage. He hoped Mrs. O'Connor would check her voice mail.

***

Olivia let Dublin know that she had picked up a strong signal from the Rivers' car as soon as she left the Longford train station in the state-of-the-art Picasso her employer had provided. Olivia fervently hoped the Rivers were not headed for County Donegal with its cliffs and scary coast roads. She was in no mood for dramatic scenery. She had had enough drama today. Robert Rivers was a formidable player. It had been *years* since Olivia had lost a trail.

***

As Robert Rivers guided the Toyota around the roundabout at Collooney, he was startled to hear a talking car computer telling him that he was on the Sligo Road, how fast he was going and that traffic was 'flowing freely' ahead. "Where did *that* come from?" he asked.

Then he froze. "How *could* I have been so *stupid?* Completely clueless!" as Liffey would say. This car he was driving had to have a tracking relationship with a satellite to get that kind of out of the blue road information. Whoever had been following him in Dublin would *certainly* have the technology to track this car. He had fled Dublin to spare Liffey from the grim reality that they were being followed, only to go back to their *bugged* rental car. Could 'they,' whoever 'they' were, intercept mobile phone calls as well? Probably. He could not risk calling his office staff in Chicago for help this time. He would have to handle this one all by himself.

Mr. Rivers looked in his review mirror and did not see anything that looked suspicious. But what would 'suspicious' *look* like? Liffey needed her ridiculous pre-feis spaghetti dinner so he would head into Sligo Town to their hotel. He would carry their luggage into the lobby, check them in and then immediately call a cab. If he could keep Liffey from leaping around practicing her steps in the lobby, probably no one would even notice them. He would then have the cab take them to *another* hotel where they would actually stay. He could only hope that the poodle lady or whoever might be following them now, would be busy parking their own car and not see the Rivers fleeing again. If he had to, he would create a diversion when it was time to go.

***

Mrs. O'Connor was *thrilled* to get the voice mail from Mr.

McFleury about the stage, although she was a bit confused because there already *was* a permanent stage made of wood in the hall. No one had mentioned to her that the judge was bringing his own stage. She had never heard of anything quite like that before. A judge with his own stage! She was sure that Mr. McFleury was an important man with 'big' connections in feiseanna circles in the U.S. and Australia. Perhaps he was a bit eccentric with an artistic temperament and all that. He certainly had a peculiar accent. She wondered if he knew Michael Flatley? He probably did if he was so well connected. She hoped that the first feis judge, who had to cancel at the last minute, was successfully recuperating after his unfortunate fishing accident. The Beltra Feis was very fortunate to have been able to secure such a prominent replacement at the last minute.

CHAPTER TWENTY-ONE

As Robert Rivers had feared, Liffey started jumping in place doing her scissor steps in the lobby as he was checking them in to the hotel. He did not think Liffey was even conscious of the fact that she rarely stood still. She was always in motion, either leaping around or jumping up and down. She never even bothered taking off her backpack when she did her practicing.

The desk clerk handed him the room key. He quickly located the concierge and asked that a cab be ordered. Mr. Rivers explained to the startled concierge that there had been a luggage mix-up and that he was going to the Strandhill Airport to straighten things out. He asked that the concierge come into the coffee shop to get them when the cab appeared.

"No need for that, sir. Here's one right now," the concierge said as he picked up their two large suitcases. Mr. Rivers grabbed his briefcase and Liffey's solo dress carrier and called out to her to join him by the front entrance.

Liffey made it to her father in three leap overs. She was perplexed to see the open back door of a *taxi cab* and even more perplexed when her father hopped in and pulled her in after him with a "Hey, how about a Sligo taxi cab comparison ride?"

This was *way* more serious than Liffey had thought. Her dad was completely off his rocker! Here they were going out for yet *another* crazy taxi cab ride. Was he going to ask *this* poor driver to do tight turns, or just see how the ride 'felt' this time? She thought better of questioning his sanity out loud, but inside she was very unsettled. What do kids do if their only parent goes nuts on them? Who do they tell? Where do they go for help? Liffey had never really had to think about things like that before.

She *could* call Aunt Jean in Chicago, but her aunt had a way of seriously over-reacting to things. Aunt Jean *might* make things worse. She might call in the Marines or something. "No, I will pretend that all this cab obsessing is normal for as long as it takes," Liffey thought, as she looked lovingly at her poor demented father.

After about a ten minute ride through Sligo Town's network of narrow, confusing streets, and then a few blocks up the river, Robert Rivers told the cab to pull up to the Riverside Hotel, and stop. Liffey could see that her father looked nervous because he kept looking behind them and from side to side like he was looking for something or somebody. But she supposed that was to be expected now that he was crazy. She would probably have to get used to all kinds of odd behavior.

Liffey was *not* prepared for the next moment, however, when he abruptly announced that they were going to *stay* at *this* hotel and that he had checked them in to the wrong hotel before.

"Daddy, the desk clerk handed you a *room key* at the other place. Don't you remember?" Liffey would have to treat her father like she was his babysitter. She would be firm, yet gentle.

"No, Liffey. I gave it back to him when you were jumping around the lobby." Liffey could not be sure if this were true or not because she *had* been practicing pretty intensely for tomorrow's feis. Maybe this *was* true. All that really concerned her now was the pre-feis spaghetti dinner. She would humor her father and his delusion that they had been in the *wrong* hotel and check into *this* hotel like this was the *right* hotel. Then she would have to find spaghetti on her own, as her father was about a minute away from a straight jacket. And this was *all* her fault! The stupid Crowning Portrait chaos she *herself* had created in London had caused her poor father to totally flip out.

"Did *you* like *this* cab ride, Daddy? *I* certainly enjoyed it," Liffey said patronizingly as she stepped out of the cab, on to the curb. Robert Rivers wondered why Liffey would ask such a weird question in such a sing-song voice. He had momentarily forgotten that he was supposed to be interested in comparing taxi cabs. "Yeah, I guess so," her father answered, obviously very preoccupied.

Liffey asked the cab driver before they went to register with the 'right' hotel where she might find some good spaghetti. To her complete joy and relief, he immediately responded: "The Bistro, or Caesar's." Then she inquired as to whether there were any late night supermarkets in Sligo because she needed to go out and buy a bagel, sliced turkey, a tomato and some cheese. "There are several," the friendly cab driver responded. Her father used to take care of the pre-feis breakfast food but he was only a shell of his former self now. If they went out again later to purchase the breakfast food, he would probably change cabs three or four times during a three block shopping mission just to compare them with the Dublin and London taxis.

Liffey decided she would walk.

***

Olivia was parked across the street from the Southern Hotel, waiting. They would *have* to come out sooner or later.

She hoped. Their car was in the hotel parking lot. Her beeper would alert her if their car ignition was engaged. She closed her eyes and drifted off to some much needed sleep in the early evening sun. It did not occur to Olivia that Robert Rivers might have simply abandoned his rental car and fled.

CHAPTER TWENTY-TWO

The pre-feis spaghetti dinner her father had delivered to their room was almost as good as the one at the Boston Meatball Palace. Almost. Not quite. Liffey felt a little ashamed of herself for doubting that Sligo would have spaghetti. There was a beautiful view of the narrow, rough Garavogue River out the window.

Robert Rivers seemed to be his old self again and was starting to think about things other than comparing taxi cabs. He pointed out that they had had a long day today and an even longer one waiting for them tomorrow and that Wee Willie Winkie would be rapping at their window any moment now. He thought the Winkie remark was pretty funny and Liffey tried to laugh appreciatively, but was worried that her father's sense of humor might be disappearing along with his sanity.

Mr. Rivers had inquired at the front desk earlier and was told that he could indeed have a proper pre-feis breakfast prepared for Liffey in the hotel dining room. He decided he would not tell Liffey and surprise her in the morning.

With Liffey's pre-feis rituals under control, Robert Rivers went about canceling his rental car and apologized to the rental agent for having to leave it in the hotel parking lot due to an unexpected emergency. Of course he realized he would have to pay an extra fee for the inconvenience this caused. He then called another car rental company and secured another car to be delivered to this hotel no later than 8:00 a.m. tomorrow morning. In the unlikely event that the new rental failed to turn up, they would get a cab out to the Beltra Feis. On the map it appeared to be approximately ten miles from their hotel.

Robert Rivers prayed the nice weather would hold so that he and Liffey could climb Knocknarea tomorrow before they left County Sligo. He had promised his wife Maeve before she died that he would take their little Anna Liffey up the mountain when she turned thirteen and play the tape-recorded message she had made for their daughter.

"Tomorrow is going to be a very important day for Liffey," he thought as sleep started to close in. He was utterly relieved that he had managed to spare Liffey from the knowledge that they were being pursued even though he was quite sure Liffey thought he was a madman now. After all, he *was* behaving like a madman! She had not screamed during the night for several weeks now. He would do anything to stop the screaming dreams forever.

***

Liffey smiled at her father snoring on the bed next to her. She was happy he could sleep. She could *not*. Tomorrow was the *next* to the biggest day of her life. The *biggest* had been getting her solo dress yesterday. Actually *wearing* the dress at a feis was almost too much to think about! She wanted to try it on again but thought it might be bad luck or something. So she resisted and instead, carefully removed it from the carrier luggage and spread it out on her bed.

She positioned the wig with the crown and tiara above the dress and sighed. She was certain that there had never been anything this exquisite designed on earth before. Maybe Middle Earth but not *this* earth. The blues were ethereal, like the fairies had made the material in secret places and used dyes made from blue cornflowers and bluebells. The Ogham letters were real silver mined by dwarves and shaped by elves. It was a magic dress made in a world hidden from mortals, maybe in one of the fairy forts that her father kept pointing out while he was driving. That had to be why it took so long to make it.

***

Liffey carefully moved the dress from her bed to the wide desk in the corner of the room. She would wear it to the feis tomorrow in case there was no place to change there. She had already done a feis bag check earlier and all of her supplies were in place. There was *no way* she was going to wear the cover-up smock. She hadn't even brought it with her because she knew her father was clueless and she could not imagine anyone from her dance school turning up and ratting on her. She supposed that there was a slight risk of someone she knew being there, but that would be a one in a billion chance.

***

Liffey looked out the window at the Garavogue River. She counted four swans who, since Liffey was in Ireland, quite possibly could be the doomed children of Lir, whose wicked stepmother had turned them into swans. When Liffey first saw the river, the big "yuk!" she let out was another opportunity for her father to launch into a lecture. This one was about blanket bogs. After he explained that the river was tea-brown because the bog water in it contains lots of tannic acid which turns water dirty brown, Liffey relaxed. She had been worried that the river was polluted and that the swans might be toxic from it. Liffey wondered if it ever actually got dark here in Ireland. It was almost 10:00 p.m. and it was still fairly light outside.

Since she needed to get the pre-feis breakfast food *and* since it was still light outside, Liffey decided *not* to wake her father up to ask him if she could walk over to the big Tesco supermarket they had passed on the way to the hotel. It was only a few blocks away and he would never even know she had gone out. He looked so peaceful, and she knew if she woke him he would only want to try out more taxi cabs and Liffey did not think she could face that again today. Tomorrow she realized she would have to act interested in cabs again, but not tonight.

She carefully slipped out of the room making sure to take a room key with her so she would not have to wake her father up when she returned.

CHAPTER TWENTY-THREE

Olivia was awakened by an annoying buzz indicating that the Rivers' rental car ignition was activated. She looked at her watch and determined she had been asleep for over three hours. She was grateful for the stretch of sleep. It was 10:20 p.m. now and still not dark.

The Rivers' car pulled out of the crowded hotel car park and into the narrow, congested street. Olivia waited so that there would be several cars between her car and the red Toyota. After only a few short blocks, it turned right into a large car park. She was directly behind the Toyota now and was careful to keep a seventy-five foot distance. Robert Rivers appeared to be alone. She assumed his daughter was back in their hotel room fast asleep. Maybe trailing the Rivers family had been a good idea after all. Robert Rivers might be making contact here in this inconspicuous parking lot with one of the other players.

Olivia watched as the Toyota parked in the far left vertical parking lane of the main lot. She was fortunate to spot an open space close to it and quickly pulled in. The driver's door opened and Olivia saw a young man alight and walk briskly towards a barely visible 'Hertz Car Rental' door in the middle of a line of small grocery stores. Her heart sank. This man was certainly *not* Robert Rivers. He looked young enough to be his son. The young man entered the tiny Hertz office and turned on the lights.

Desperately hoping she had not again lost the Rivers and that there was a rational explanation for this man driving their car, she hastily followed the young man into the Hertz office. "Sorry, we're closed," he said cheerfully. "Oh, I realize that," Olivia replied just as cheerfully. "I just wanted to inquire as to whether or not the Toyota you just parked might be available for a friend of mine to rent tomorrow morning." "As a matter of fact, it will be," he answered. "It was just released. Some people don't seem to have any problem with flushing money down the toilet. I told the man there was a penalty fee for not returning the car to the same place where he had rented it, and he said 'no problem' and that he would pay extra to leave the car here in Sligo instead of driving it back to the airport in Dublin. He said his plans had changed unexpectedly."

Olivia felt weak and sick to her stomach. Dublin would have to be notified. They would tell ICOM and then there would be the French and who knows *who* else involved. This could get way out of hand very quickly. Olivia decided she needed to eat something before she could face advising Dublin that she had messed up again. As soon as she called in and told them, she would be history. She wasn't paid to mess up.

The Tesco was open and Olivia headed towards it in a fog of confusion and disbelief. She could not understand *how* she had let them get away *twice* in one day. Something to eat would clear her head. Then she would make the call to Dublin and Dublin would call London and London would call France and France might call *everybody*.

As Olivia walked into the Tesco store, she passed by a young girl at a check out counter who appeared to be doing some kind of tap dance in place. Olivia smiled. The young lady obviously did not care that people were staring at her.

She didn't seem to notice. She was totally preoccupied with whatever it was she was practicing.

Olivia selected two chocolate bars to fuel her depleted spirits and looked again at the intense young girl who was now jumping in place while she received her change from a bemused cashier.

The girl looked familiar. It was then that Olivia knew what a last minute reprieve from the electric chair must feel like. This wide-eyed young lady was the daughter of Robert Rivers.

Olivia tried to imagine *how* Liffey Rivers had managed to evade her father and go on a late-night shopping expedition all by herself. After all the trouble he had gone through to slip away from Olivia's tracking them, she was *certain* Robert Rivers did not know his daughter was out on the town. He was most likely fast asleep, exhausted from his long cat-and-mouse day. Olivia would follow Liffey back to wherever it was she and Robert Rivers were now staying and keep vigil. It wasn't time yet to make a move. Doing nothing most of the time was the most strenuous part of the world in which Olivia lived.

***

Mrs. O'Connor was so thrilled to meet Mr. McFleury that she initially had difficulty speaking. He was much better looking than she had expected with his wavy, prematurely white hair, and he was very charming. The fact that she could not quite place his accent made him all the more mysterious. To think he cared so much about the dancers he was to judge tomorrow that he had transported his stage all the way over here from England, and at his own cost! She was glad she had been able to find some strong men to help him get the stage into the hall.

CHAPTER TWENTY-FOUR

Robert Rivers woke up on Saturday morning and saw his daughter happily munching on a bagel piled with turkey and melted cheese and topped with a tomato slice. "Well good morning, Ms. Rivers," he said cheerfully. "I see that you managed to get the kitchen to serve you the preventative jinx breakfast while I was sleeping."

He saw the quick flash of confusion on Liffey's pre-feis face. Liffey did not like to lie. She thought lies should be reserved for occasions when there was no way the truth could be told. Like if her really dorky cousin Leonard came over to visit and she would say "It's really *nice* to see you, Leonard," knowing fully well she *totally* wished he had *not* come over for a visit because he was so *boring*.

Liffey was not going to lie to her father about a bagel. "Daddy, I don't think I know what you're talking about. While you were asleep last night, *before* it got dark, I walked a few blocks to the 24-hour Tesco and bought everything I needed for the feis breakfast. I asked at the front desk and they told me it was safe. I didn't want to wake you up and see you start riding around in taxi cabs again and you looked so peaceful and you *never told* me I could not go outside without you. You have always said how *safe* this part of Ireland is. I am *really* sorry if I did something to upset you," Liffey concluded.

Liffey saw the look of shock on her father's face and quickly added: "*Nothing happened*, Daddy. All I did was buy the jinx-stopper breakfast stuff and walk right back to the hotel. I only stopped to watch the swans for a few minutes. There were four of them like in the *Children of Lir* story. No one threatened me and there were lots of people on the street."

Robert Rivers could not let Liffey see at this point, just a few hours before the long-awaited Beltra Feis, how utterly defeated he felt that after *all* of the safeguard taxi cab measures he had taken to dodge whoever it was that was following them, Liffey had innocently put herself in harm's way. She seemed to have a pattern of doing that. He realized that there was nothing he could do *now* about whether or not Liffey had been spotted last night. He would have to hope that she had *not* been recognized and that the day ahead of them would be relatively disaster free. And stay on guard.

***

Mr. McFleury arrived at Beltra Hall two hours ahead of checking in time. He had asked Mrs. O'Connor to give him a key to get in because he had told her he needed to do his meditation exercises several hours prior to the competition's commencing and that he also needed to pray about the judging he was going to do and ask for 'wisdom from above' to judge wisely. She was almost moved to tears thinking about how dedicated he was and how lucky they were to get such a judge here in Sligo. She gave him the key. He was now safely inside the hall, all alone, setting up. It was 7:00 a.m. He was to supervise the stage pick-up after the feis at 2:00 p.m. His beloved stage would then be driven to Killybegs in County Donegal, weighted down and dumped at sea from a fishing trawler. There would be no forensic experts examining *his* stage for hairs, fibers, chemicals and whatever.

CHAPTER TWENTY-FIVE

It was time to get dressed. Liffey's father was in the lobby checking them out. Liffey was to meet him down there when she was ready to leave. He would be having his coffee in the lounge and said that there was no rush. He was waiting for the new rental car to arrive. It was 8:15 a.m. and the car was late.

Liffey tried very hard not to be nervous but she was very, *very* tense. True enough, her father was losing it and she was about to make a fool out of herself in front of *real* Irish dancers, but there was more. She could *not* shake the feeling that something else was very *wrong* with today. She felt shivery and prickly, like before a storm that brings lots of lightning and thunder. Liffey was always anxious before dancing at a feis but this was different. She felt afraid deep down inside and there was no explanation for it. On the plus side, the weather was gorgeous today so she and her father would be able to climb Knocknarea after she danced *and* she was about to put on the most beautiful dress in the whole wide world. Yet she could not shake this feeling of dread.

Liffey did some serious stretching and then pulled on the only-worn-one-other-time poodle socks and laced up her ghillies. Like the spaghetti noodles, she had also forgotten her sock glue and was planning to buy some later from a feis vendor before she danced. Carefully slipping into her very first solo dress, Liffey closed her eyes, savoring the moment and imagining how perfect it would be if her mother could only be here now to zip it up.

***

Olivia had seen the sallow faced man with the slicked back hair fifteen minutes ago in the coffee shop. He had been reading a newspaper and nibbling on toast. Olivia picked up a vibe and did the 'stand up and leave quickly test' and he too stood up and left. Now she was sitting in her Picasso across from the hotel and she noted that he was having another cup of coffee in the *same place* that they had both just exited. He was *definitely* following her. But why? She was certain that Dublin had never found out about her having lost the Rivers twice yesterday. They could only know about the first time. She doubted that the Rivers were being double-teamed by her own syndicate. He had to be working for someone else. Olivia profoundly hoped that he was not armed. She took the compact revolver out of her bag and double checked that it was loaded.

It was loaded. It was 8:30 a.m.

***

At 8:40 a.m., Liffey Rivers did a final inspection in the mirror. There was someone else looking back at her. Someone who was *confident* and ready for anything! "This is solo dress magic," Liffey thought as she applied some clear lip gloss.

Liffey slipped her feet into the oversized clogs she had remembered to pack to protect her leather ghillies as she walked. She took a deep breath, and double-checked her dance bag to make sure she had her inhaler and water bottle and left the room.

When Liffey reached the hotel lobby, she saw her father talking with the concierge by the front entrance. Then she saw the waiting cab. "Great! Here we go again!" Liffey sighed. Her father had seemed relatively normal this morning and she had forgotten all about his new obsession with taxi cabs.

"Liffey, you look like a princess!" Robert Rivers exclaimed. Liffey smiled, bracing herself for what she knew was coming next. "Guess what? The rental company called and said our car cannot be delivered until 10:00 a.m. So they volunteered to pay for a cab to get us out to Beltra." "Wonderful," Liffey replied mechanically as the concierge opened the door.

***

As the taxi left the hotel, Liffey noticed a forest green car pulling out across the street heading in the opposite direction. She also noticed her father's reaction. Robert Rivers' posture changed ever so slightly as he caught a glimpse of auburn hair and sunglasses passing by. Liffey thought her father's jumpy demeanor was due to the fact that he must be already mentally comparing today's Sligo cab with the cabs in London and Dublin.

"Daddy, do you want me to take notes for you about this taxi while we are driving to Beltra? I have a notebook and pen in my dance bag. You can just say what you think and I will write it all down for you."

Liffey would have to handle her father's craziness sooner or later. But since the feis was *sooner*, she would prefer to handle her poor father's madness *later. After* the feis! Liffey tried not to think about how anxious she was about the stupid Hornpipe. She *hated* it more than she hated 'former' and 'latter.'

"*Why* would I want you to take notes about this taxi, Liffey?" her father asked innocently. He did not seem to be concentrating on the cab thing at the moment, so Liffey tried to distract him, even at the risk of a history lecture.

"Daddy, what is that weird-looking flat man sculpture?" she asked as they drove across the Garavogue River and made a sharp left turn after the bridge. "That's William Butler Yeats, Liffey, Ireland's greatest poet. He won the Nobel Prize for literature in the early 1920's and put Ireland on the map in literary circles. He also helped start the Abbey Theatre in Dublin. You would like his poetry. Some historians say that he believed in fairies and there are lots of references to them in his poetry. He spent much of his childhood in Sligo, and Sligo is very proud of him. In fact, he mentions Knocknarea in one of his poems and I even know a few verses from it!" Liffey braced herself hoping that a *few* verses did not mean fifty.

Robert Rivers finished his Yeats lecture by telling Liffey that probably the best known of Yeats' poems is *The Lake Isle of Innisfree*. "Like the perfume I saw at the airport?" asked Liffey. "Precisely, answered her father. I will buy it for you before we head back to Chicago if you promise to learn the first few verses." "Sure," Liffey agreed. "Thanks, Daddy." "The island is about five miles from where we are now. The next time we come to Sligo, we will do the boat tour and get out there to see it."

They drove past a huge building that looked like a courthouse. Robert Rivers kept looking in the driver's rear view mirror. Liffey was preoccupied with going over her dance steps with her fingers on the back seat of the cab.

Olivia kept a two-block distance between her Picasso and the taxi.

The sallow faced man also kept a two-block distance between his Ford and Olivia's Picasso. The Rivers' 'parade' headed towards Beltra. It was 8:50 a.m.

CHAPTER TWENTY-SIX

The scenery on the way to the Beltra Feis was so beautiful that Liffey temporarily forgot about how worried she was that she would make a fool of herself in just a few more hours. There were the Ox Mountains and Ballysadare Bay and ancient stone walls and shimmering green fields with grazing sheep and tunnels of trees and even a pointy mountain that looked like a pyramid.

Liffey was concerned that after her father had finished his Yeats lecture, he had just *stopped* talking. He wasn't even commenting on the almost mystical looking countryside that went streaking by them in the speeding cab. Liffey knew that there were ringforts and tombs and castle ruins and all *kinds* of things along this route that normally would have sent her father into an historical frenzy.

But there was not one word from him. She feared that he was either sick or so absorbed in his weird taxi cab world that he didn't even *notice* all the incredible stuff that they normally would have been discussing. As much as she sometimes dreaded her father's lectures, she would have loved one now about this beautiful Irish landscape. Liffey noticed again that although he tried not to show it, he was still looking into the driver's rear view mirror about every thirty seconds. What was he looking for?

***

Olivia distinctly saw the man with the pasty complexion again at the Ballysadare roundabout. He was directly behind her. For someone who was supposedly covertly following her, he certainly did not seem to be keeping much distance between their two cars.

***

The man behind Olivia knew he was being careless. He did not much care though whether or not the woman in the green Picasso was aware that he was tailing her. It might actually be helpful in the long run if she *did* know. It would make her edgy and hence less efficient. Part of his 'job description' today was to make sure that the woman in the car in front of him did not sabotage the exchange. He was under orders to use force if necessary. He suspected that she did not even know where the Rivers were headed and that she was just tracking their movements. He *did* know where the Rivers were going because he had done his homework. That dancer girl might have discovered that the National Portrait Gallery in London had a missing painting, but she could not know anything else. It was his job to keep it that way.

***

The cab driver announced that they were almost at Beltra Hall. It was 9:10 a.m. Liffey could see an elderly man ahead who was directing traffic from the main road into the parking lot. She was glad that there were not a zillion cars lined up waiting to enter the lot like at the Chicago Feis.

The taxi dropped them off in front of the small, somewhat gloomy, red-barn-like building. There was nothing Irish, or for that matter even *interesting* about Beltra Hall. It had none of the rustic beauty of the buildings Liffey had viewed while driving in from Sligo Town. Robert Rivers said it first, "Hmm, this place is pretty dreary, Liff." Liffey thought so too. She was disappointed that a feis in Ireland could look so nondescript. She did not know exactly *what* she had expected, but it certainly was *not* this little place. It reminded her of her dull Irish dance school dress.

The melancholy mood Beltra Hall projected outside faded, however, when Liffey entered the building. There were two adorable old ladies checking in the dancers. They were obviously excited about the upcoming feis and unlike some of the grouchy check-in people Liffey had encountered in the States, they looked like there was no where else on earth that they would rather be than right here checking in the dancers. Their eyes sparkled as they told Liffey that she was "very welcome indeed" and then they wished her good luck. One of the women asked where she came from in the States, and then even pretended to have heard of Wisconsin. "Ah, you had such a long journey." When the woman said "Ah," she gasped, sucking in air, so that Liffey at first was afraid she was about to choke. But she didn't.

For some reason unknown to Liffey, her father had positioned himself at the front door of Beltra Hall like he was expecting someone or something. Liffey didn't mind. He was probably thinking about their cab ride in from Sligo Town or wondering if the new rental car was going to turn up.

***

The feis judge, Mr. McFleury, was talking to Mrs. O'Connor at his stage. She was admiring it and telling him that it was very, very kind of him to be so solicitous. He smiled and told her that not only was this stage *safe*, but it was also a *research* center. Mrs. O'Connor looked confused. He went on to explain: "Under this stage, I have installed sophisticated equipment to measure the velocity of the average dancer with regard to their hard shoe steps. Before this stage leaves today, I shall retrieve the electroplate panel and then analyze the data back in my office."

Mrs. O'Connor was very impressed. Not only was Mr. McFleury a sensitive, *artistic* man, evidently he was also a *scientist*. She agreed to help him remove the delicate research panel prior to the stage being shipped back to England after the feis.

***

Liffey moved into the small hall, studying her feis registration number which, in her opinion, was not at all lucky. Her number today was 25. Liffey always hoped for a feis number that was numerically in order counting both ways, like a 123, or backwards, 321. She would just have to make the best of it with this unlucky number. At least she could not think of any reason the number 25 would be jinxed. If she did well today, she might even revise her lucky and unlucky number system.

Liffey noticed that the hall was set up very peculiarly. There was a real stage at the end of the hall but it was not being used. Instead, there was a platform stage like the ones she was used to dancing on, which was taking up most of the room's width. There were chairs set up on either side of the stage for spectators.

Before Liffey could find a seat and settle in, a girl who was wearing a lovely pink solo dress, and who appeared to be about Liffey's age, came up and introduced herself. "Hi-ya! I'm Sinead. I'm meant to be looking after you. My mum found out a dancer from the States was coming over and wanted to make sure you would be taken care of properly."

Liffey was thrilled. She never expected dancers at feiseanna to actually *talk* to her! It usually felt more like everybody was always checking everybody else out.

Liffey braced herself and announced her own name. "I'm Liffey Rivers."

"Do you mean like the river in Dublin?" Sinead asked. At last! Someone who actually *knew* where her namesake's river was! She would not be called Shannon today! "That is really cool," Sinead said. "I wish I had an interesting name. *Everybody* here is named Sinead. Say, have you got a look at the 'twinky' judge yet? He's *winking* at everyone like some kind of head case."

"*Winking* at everyone?" asked Liffey. "That's really weird. In the States, judges don't even make eye contact with dancers when they're not dancing."

"Oh it's the same way, here," Sinead said. "But this guy is totally mad! He's winking at all the dancers and says hello to everybody too."

"Where's he from?" Liffey asked. "No one seems to know," Sinead replied. "Mrs. O'Connor says she is fairly certain he is a good friend of Michael Flatley but Mrs. O'Connor pretty much lives in her own world," Sinead snickered.

"Oh, I forgot to tell you the *best* part! The judge brought his *own stage* with him all the way from England! Can you even believe anyone would be that nuts? He hauled it over on the ferry from Holyhead just to make sure none of us slips and falls, is what he told Mrs. O'Connor. The guy is crazy."

Liffey had to agree with Sinead that the judge was very strange. All at once, Liffey realized she was having a really good time with Sinead and did not much care if or even *when* the dancing started.

"Oh-I forgot. I need to buy some sock glue," Liffey said.

"From where?" Sinead asked. "Like from a vendor," Liffey explained. "A vendor? Here in Beltra? I think a vendor turned up *once*, but this is such a small feis they don't bother to come normally." "Great, I guess my socks will be dancing then too!" Liffey moaned.

"I have sock glue. You can use mine," Sinead offered.

"Am I making an actual *friend*?" thought Liffey. It was too much to hope for. Sinead would probably disappear as soon as her own friends arrived. But Liffey was delighted to have the company for the moment.

As Sinead went off to collect her dance bag and get the sock glue, Liffey craned her neck to get a better look at the judge who was sitting at his little desk winking at anyone wearing a dance costume who would look at him.

The little beginner dancers were deliberately running up to the front of his station trying to get him to wink again and again at them. Then they would run off giggling. Their mothers were beginning to look perplexed.

Liffey shivered a little. She did not sense 'friendly' from this 'winking judge.' He gave her the creeps and there was something that seemed familiar about him too. "But that's impossible," Liffey concluded.

CHAPTER TWENTY-SEVEN

Liffey waved to her father, who was still posted at the door like some kind of security guard. He could watch her dance from there but he was certainly acting strangely again today.

***

Olivia parked the Picasso across the street from the hall in a farmer's field designated for overflow parking. She carefully avoided the front door of the hall and casually walked around the building and positioned herself at a side window which gave her a good view inside.

She did not know much about Irish dancing but she gathered that this was a competition and that is why the Rivers girl had been jumping up and down in the Tesco last night. She had been practicing.

Olivia could not help thinking that following Robert Rivers and his bouncing daughter around was ridiculous. But then *why*, when he sensed he was being followed, did he take such *extreme* evasive measures if he did *not* have something to hide? Olivia had been on many wild goose chases during her career. This was probably just the same old thing and *anyone* would flee if they thought someone was following them. "I certainly would," she thought, thinking of the man in the coffee shop and that perhaps she had better be looking out for *herself* while she tracked the Rivers today.

***

The sallow faced man passed right by Beltra Hall and then doubled back. He parked in an open space right in back of the hall. He needed to get inside to position himself to make sure he would be able to act quickly if the Picasso lady tried to interfere. The exchange was to take place at noon during the diversion. It should all go according to plan. Mr. Smith, he had been told, was a pro.

***

Liffey asked Sinead when it would be time for them to dance. Sinead looked around the room and told Liffey it would probably be around noon because there were twenty beginners today and they would not be dancing until the beginners had finished. It was almost 10:30 a.m. and long past the time for the feis to begin.

There was a tin whistle player warming up to accompany the beginners. "We get a concertina," Sinead said. "The penny whistle is for the younger dancers. It's easier for them to keep count with the whistle."

The Irish National Anthem began playing over the speaker system. Everybody stood up and sang along. Liffey tried to follow but the words were all in Irish and her vocabulary was limited to words about fairies and ghosts.

After the anthem, Mrs. O'Connor introduced the feis with a few words: "Welcome all and thank you for your support! We are ready to begin now but first I would like to introduce you to our renowned judge for today's feis, Donald McFleury."

"Isn't that a *dessert?*" asked Liffey giggling. Sinead got it and laughed too. Mr. McFleury stood up and waved at the crowd like he was waving to his fan club. Then he winked and bowed his head modestly.

Liffey and Sinead could hardly control their laughter. He

was absolutely *absurd*! This feis suddenly seemed like a big party instead of a nerve-wracking competition.

The first two beginners took their place on stage in front of Mr. McFleury. He winked a few times at them and the tin whistle started playing. One of the little girls started crying and ran off the stage to her mother. Mr. McFleury looked distraught. The other beginner did not miss a beat and continued dancing her jig.

Liffey noticed that Mr. McFleury did not seem to be making any notes as each group of dancers danced. She wondered how he could later score the dancers if he wrote nothing down. "Maybe they do it differently over here," she thought.

Liffey could see that her father was no longer at the front door and assumed he had gone out to sign for the new rental car. It was 11:25.

Mrs. O'Connor announced there would be a short break while the beginners had their scores tallied. "What *scores?*" Liffey asked Sinead. "Did you see him write *anything* down while the dancers danced?" "No, I didn't," Sinead said.

The room was quieted ten minutes later by Mrs. O'Connor. "Beginners, please come forward and take your place on stage for your results." Mr. McFleury handed the results sheet to Mrs. O'Connor who read aloud: "In first place we have dancer number 10."

It was little Aisling Murphy. There was a collective gasp. Then quiet. Then scant applause and muttering.

Sinead informed Liffey that "Aisling Murphy is the little beginner who ran off the stage to her mother in tears and didn't even dance one bar of eight."

Second and third places were equally surprising for the crowd. It was as if Mr. McFleury had just picked any old numbers and assigned places. It was *almost* as if he did not know *what he was doing.*

Mrs. O'Connor was mobbed by future diva mothers and tried to troubleshoot but she needed to call the advanced dancers to take their places. She was certain that Mr. McFleury must have had his *reasons* for scoring so unusually. She would ask him to explain after the feis.

Sinead and Liffey heard Mrs. O'Connor's order to line up and eagerly took their place. The feis was proceeding at record speed. It was not even 11:45 a.m.

There were only six advanced dancers. This was the smallest feis Liffey had ever heard of and she was not sure where or how she fit in.

She was sure there were no preliminary or open championship levels at today's feis because there had to be three judges for those levels. There just seemed to be this one advanced 'Prizewinner' level and Liffey was not even nervous because Mr. McFleury was so bizarre and Sinead was so much fun. If you could get a first place here for not even dancing, maybe she could get a medal too!

Liffey cased the crowd and saw that her father was *still* at the door. She also saw a man with a pasty face standing against the back wall. "That guy seriously needs some sun," Liffey thought. It was 11:50 a.m.

The concertina man appeared to be ready to play his instrument. Liffey and Sinead would dance together. Sinead was a bit more advanced than Liffey, but Liffey was delighted to be dancing with a friend. Even if her friend *was* a better dancer!

They were second in line. The first pair of dancers in Liffey's group tried hard not to laugh as they took their places and Mr. McFleury winked at them. Liffey was very grateful that they were not all lining up at this Beltra Feis on the stage (as they usually did in the States), while the other dancers did their steps. Then she would have to look at Mr. McFleury while he was winking at the other dancers and she did not trust herself not to break up with laughter.

The first two dancers finished their Jigs. Liffey had good Jig steps and was anxious to do them. She squeezed Sinead's hand for good luck as they started on to the stage. The first two dancers rolled their eyes at them as they passed by. Liffey bit her lip. She would *have* to control herself or people might think she was a rude foreigner. She must *not* laugh. It was 11: 57 a.m.

CHAPTER TWENTY-EIGHT

When Liffey stepped on to the special stage, she felt little prickles in her feet. It was difficult to walk. Was there an electrical outlet wiring problem? Sinead looked untouched as she pointed her right foot and stiffened her arms next to her body. "This has to be in my head. Sinead is fine. There is no electrical problem with this stage. The *problem* is my own pathetic brain," Liffey told herself and she too pointed her right foot.

The concertina music began. Liffey began to count, trying to ignore the pins and needles which had now begun to run up and down her spine. With great will power, hoping the judge would not wink at her and make her laugh, Liffey *made* herself look into Mr. McFleury's eyes to establish the judge-dancer 'connection' her dance instructors were always talking about.

Adjudicator McFleury did not wink at Liffey who grabbed on to Sinead and *screamed*!

"Daddy, it's *him*! *It's the skunk man*! *Daddy! Daddy!*" Liffey shrieked with accelerating volume. She was paralyzed with fear, unable to either move her body or take her eyes away from Mr. McFleury's vicious stare. Sinead did her best to hold up Liffey, who was trembling and wheezing and beginning to slump down to the ground.

Robert Rivers bounded on to the stage and scooped Liffey into his arms. Her breathing was labored and all the color had drained from her face. "Liffey, I'm here. You are *fine*. Do you hear me? You are just *fine*."

Complete pandemonium had broken out in the small hall.

Mr. McFleury was a *skunk?* How ridiculous.

What was *wrong* with that poor young American girl? Beautiful solo dress though.

How could anyone be *afraid* of that nice, if somewhat odd, little man?

Mrs. O'Connor ran to Mr. McFleury to comfort him and assured him they would take care of the unfortunate dancer who obviously had something not quite right about her.

"Can I help?" Sinead asked Robert Rivers anxiously. "Yes. Please bring me her dance bag so I can get her inhaler," Robert Rivers answered as he carried Liffey off the platform stage and back to the other stage in the hall. A feis mother offered a blanket and pillow.

Mrs. O'Connor was telling everyone that the emergency was being handled and to please calm down and that things would start up again momentarily.

"Daddy," Liffey whispered breathlessly, "Daddy. *He* took it."

"Took what, Liffey?"

"The Queen Elizabeth I portrait. *I know it Daddy! That's* why I got the pins and needles in the art gallery. I didn't tell you about them in London because it didn't make any sense to me then. But it *does now.* They were *warning* me about the skunk man. The pins and needles were *telling* me I was in *danger* and I didn't pay any attention to them. He has the portrait right *here.* I think it's under the stage and that's why I'm all prickly now."

"Liffey, you are all prickly now because you are not getting enough oxygen. Wait until you get your inhaler. Then you can tell me why you think this man is the same one who threatened you in St. Louis."

Sinead arrived with the inhaler and knelt down on the stage, carefully re-arranging Liffey on the pillow. Liffey sat up, inhaled the chemicals, and immediately began to relax as she started to breathe again normally.

***

Olivia looked through the window while she pretended to be smoking a cigarette. She was not a smoker. Smoke made her sick to her stomach but she had to have a logical reason to be hanging around outside this event staring through a window.

She was worried about the Rivers girl and wondered if she were ill. Olivia couldn't hear what Liffey had been screaming when she had the meltdown. Something about a skunk and a man? Her father had taken her to the other stage and she was temporarily out of Olivia's sight. Olivia thought again how absurd it was that she was following this man and his Irish dancer daughter all over Ireland.

Unexpectedly, Olivia was cold and shivery even though the sun was hot. She looked into the hall again and spotted the coffee shop man inside *watching* the judge. What was *he* doing in there? If he was *just* following her for *whatever* reason, he would not be in the hall blending in with the crowd. It was obvious he was not a daddy looking for his little dancer. This man was trouble. "He must have been following me because he knew *I was following* Robert Rivers and his daughter."

Olivia took out her mobile and checked in with Dublin. Her fears mounted when she was told that Interpol had put out a code green on this operation. That meant she was probably only an hour away, if *that*, from the arrival in little Beltra of agents from all over Europe. She had to get inside and be on top of *whatever* it was that was going to go down in there.

***

The coffee shop man moved into position. That crazy dancer had just called way too much attention to Mr. Smith. They would have to move faster now, before things here got completely out of control. He could not hear what the girl was saying to the man at the other end of the hall but his instincts said to *move now.*

***

Mr. McFleury told Mrs. O'Connor that he had heart problems and that the unpleasant screaming incident had given him chest pains. He suggested that they start the feis again immediately as there were only five more dancers to judge including the unfortunate one who had been dancing with the girl who had called him a skunk. He needed to get rest, but was determined to finish his adjudicator responsibilities. Mrs. O'Connor went about collecting the dancers and trying to re-establish an organized front. Mr. McFleury recognized the sallow-faced man wearing the green tie and blue suit jacket. The green tie man yawned and stretched. That was the signal. It was time.

Mr. McFleury reached under his judging desk and pushed a button. In five minutes there would be so much smoke in Beltra Hall that everyone would have to flee. Mr. McFleury would not let himself think about the fact that the little wig-head menace was here, and once again causing major problems for him. He pressed the release button under the stage and his 'electroplated research center' dropped two inches on to the tracks and rolled forward, stopping within arm reach.

***

"Sinead, you *have* to go back and dance," Liffey implored her new friend. "No way," Sinead replied. "I'm staying right here with you."

"Liffey," Robert Rivers began. "If you are absolutely *positive* that the Queen Elizabeth portrait is hidden under the stage, then I am going to call the police. We cannot handle this alone. You need to be absolutely certain though that the warning signals are telling you that the portrait is here and that you are not just *imagining* that this adjudicator is the same man who threatened you in St. Louis."

"I'm sure, Daddy," Liffey answered firmly. Liffey was very thankful her father took her seriously. He had learned, as had Liffey, to rely on the pins and needles premonition warnings that came to her out of the blue.

Liffey was terrified the skunk man would harm her but at the same time, she knew her father would protect her. Liffey was well aware that this was the *second* time she found herself in the middle of one of his smuggling schemes. She couldn't *believe* it was happening again. She held her father's hand tightly. Robert Rivers dialed emergency and explained who he was and that there was a critical situation at the Beltra Feis.

In a low voice, he warned the police that there might be a gun involved because the feis judge was a dangerous man who was intending to fence the Queen Elizabeth I portrait which he had stolen from the National Portrait Gallery in London and had hidden in the feis stage.

"Well," thought Robert Rivers, fully realizing how completely crazy his phone call must have sounded, "the garda dispatcher will either send the police or have me removed and institutionalized for emergency mental health care."

***

The concertina player gave an introduction and the next two dancers took their places as if nothing had happened. Mr. McFleury no longer winked at the dancers. He sat like a tense cat waiting to spring on an unsuspecting bird.

The diversion hit just as the dancers launched themselves into their Reel steps. There was a loud hissing noise like a giant can of soda exploding. Then there was so much smoke it was difficult to see anything.

Mrs. O'Connor, who had been standing next to the microphone, gave emergency directions in a remarkably calm voice: "Do not panic. Do *not* run. Walk slowly and carefully to the exit nearest you. Then move quickly *away* from the door and by *all* means, do *not* *block* the exit doors. Move away from the building but *not* into the road. Walk *left* when you exit the building into the parking lot and be sure you locate your children and then keep them with you. Remember there is also a door at the rear of this building. If your child is not with you, we will find her or him. We will not leave the hall until we are certain no one is left behind. This smoke does not appear to be related to a fire and it does not appear to be life-threatening."

Mrs. O'Connor had five grown sons and was fairly certain that this smoke was someone's sick idea of a prank. She recognized a peculiar odor which she had not smelled since her boys thought stink bombs were hilarious a long, long time ago.

***

Olivia ran to the back door instinctively, revolver in hand. If the man was going to be leaving the building with someone or something, she was going to see what he was up to. Was he after the girl? Was this a *kidnapping* attempt in progress? Olivia had been told that Robert Rivers was a wealthy man.

Olivia reached the door seconds before the coffee shop man exited, his face covered with a wet handkerchief. He was obviously prepared for the smoke. He was alone. Olivia flattened herself into the shadows of the building.

***

Mrs. O'Connor rushed to Mr. McFleury who also had wet his handkerchief with the bottled water provided by the feis committee and covered his face. She was worried about his heart and his research panel. He was removing the electroplated velocity panel when she arrived. "Here, he choked. Please be so kind as to take this out the back door, Mrs. O'Connor. I am afraid I am a little weak-kneed."

Mrs. O'Connor was happy to help protect the research and easily carried the ten pound panel out the back door. She was met there by a man in a green tie and blue suit coat jacket.

"I'll hold this for you madam while you make sure everybody gets out safely." Mrs. O'Connor gratefully accepted the kind stranger's offer thinking how nice it was in situations like this when everybody pulled together.

***

Robert Rivers came through the back door directly after the mysterious man. He was carrying Liffey whose asthma had worsened again in the smoke. Sinead was with them holding the inhaler up like a fire extinguisher. Liffey perked up immediately in the fresh air.

"Daddy, you have to save the portrait!" she cried out when she saw the man who needed some sun walking away with a wooden panel.

***

Olivia had watched the wooden panel exchange from the shadows.

"This all seems way too 'been-there-done-that,'" Liffey reflected, as she helplessly watched the man with the Queen Elizabeth I white skin *effortlessly* escaping with what must be the priceless portrait of the queen.

Robert Rivers could not leave Liffey alone not knowing the whereabouts of the skunk man. He believed Liffey when she told him that she had recognized the skunk man masquerading as the feis judge. It made sense. The skunk man was an international criminal. "Diamonds, now art and who knows *what else?*" Robert Rivers thought. Both men were probably armed and he *knew* they were dangerous. He needed to stay right by Liffey's side and hope that the gardai would arrive in time to give chase to the thief.

Liffey impulsively made up her mind to try to rescue the portrait herself. Knowing that her father would *totally* forbid her to even stand up now let alone try to stop the thief, she stood up quickly and started yelling: "*Stop that man!* He's *got stolen art* inside that panel he's carrying! He's a *thief*! Somebody *stop* him!"

Robert Rivers was shocked. He did not think Liffey had enough air inside her lungs to make so much noise. He swiftly pushed Liffey back down to the ground with Sinead and shielded them both with his body in case the man was armed.

To Liffey's utter astonishment, she had *back up*! A woman stepped out of the building's shadows, aimed a GUN and barked: "Stop right where you are, sir! Put the panel *down* on the ground and lift your hands up high above your head. I have a gun. I am an Interpol agent and you are under arrest."

A faint sound of approaching sirens could be heard in the distance. The man dropped the panel and *ran*! Olivia let him go. She would let the Sligo Gardai apprehend the fleeing thief.

Liffey fearfully reminded her father that the skunk man was still at large as he and Olivia carefully retrieved the panel. Sinead sat loyally next to Liffey with the inhaler.

Robert Rivers asked Olivia to search the hall in case the adjudictor had not managed to escape during all the confusion and was hiding inside. But Robert Rivers knew that there was no point because by now, Mr. McFleury, or whoever he was, was not going to be anywhere *near* Beltra Hall. The sirens were much closer now. It would only be a matter of seconds until help arrived.

Olivia walked tentatively into the building, holding her gun and aiming it at the floor. The acrid smoke had entirely cleared out. There were two feis volunteers inside tidying up. They stopped sweeping the floor and huddled together when they saw the attractive, *armed* woman looking at them.

"*No*, please leave everything just as it is!" Olivia directed. "This is a crime scene and there will soon be teams of forensic experts and detectives examining every inch of this place. I must ask you to leave the premises at once so as not to disturb any evidence that might have been left behind."

One of the workers told Olivia that Mrs. O'Connor had driven the adjudicator, Mr. McFleury, to the hospital when he had been 'overcome' by the smoke.

Sinead and Liffey exchanged e-mail addresses and Liffey promised to call her right away when she got back to the States.

CHAPTER TWENTY-NINE

Liffey and her father were more than half way up Knocknarea now.

They could clearly see the mountains of Donegal and Ben Bulben and the Ox Mountains and the Celtic-like-spirals the tide left behind decorating the beaches.

Beneath the Ox Mountains, in Beltra Hall, detectives and teams of international forensic experts were inspecting Mr. McFleury's stage.

Outside the hall there were television cameras and news reporters and poor Mrs. O'Connor who had lost Adjudicator McFleury in the parking lot of Sligo General Hospital.

She explained that she had driven him there for smoke inhalation therapy and that he had a heart condition and that she was *very* worried about him because when she got out of the driver's seat of his rental car, he had moved over from the passenger side and just driven off all by himself without even waving good-bye! The smoke had obviously impaired his brain and Mrs. O'Connor thought that the gardai should be out trying to find *him* instead of asking *her* all these questions. He must have had an extra set of car keys, Mrs. O'Connor said.

"No." She could not remember what color the car was. It might have been blue or green or purple. "No." She did not know what make of car it was either. It might have been a Ford or Peugot or an Opal.

***

"It would be like cloud climbing," Liffey thought as she and her father reached the top of Knocknarea mountain, and gazed *upward* at the seventy-five-foot high pile of zillions of rocks and little stones they were about to ascend. Clouds obscured the summit. "Watch your step, Liff," her father advised. "This cairn has been here for over five thousand years but people like us add a stone every time they come up here and it gets a little slippery sometimes," Robert Rivers pointed out, as he dropped his small stone at the bottom of the passage tomb. Liffey was waiting to place her stone at the very *top*.

Climbing in the clouds made Liffey feel like she was standing on the highest point on earth.

"Knocknarea is slightly more than a thousand feet high, Liffey, but it seems much higher, doesn't it?" Liffey could tell that Robert Rivers was ready for his 'top of the mountain lecture.' "Queen Maeve's grave is at the highest point," he continued.

When Liffey climbed the east-side trail to the top of the huge cairn, the western wind struck her full in the face. She quickly turned her back to the ocean and the wind, and drew in her breath in an "Ah" gasp, like the lady who had welcomed her to the Beltra Feis.

The clouds had parted. Spread before her, in an enormous half-circle, for as far as she could see without turning her head from left to right, was what looked like all the mountains in the world. Ben Bulben was on the left, with its ocean-facing cliff looking like the prow of an enormous ship steaming into the Atlantic. From Ben Bulben, the mountains swept without a break across the sky.

She could see on some of the peaks that there were other great cairns, like the one she stood upon. She marveled at the cairns, these things that her ancestors had built so long ago, and added her pebble.

The climb down the cairn was a bit more difficult than climbing up. Robert Rivers suggested that they find a comfortable rock to sit on and Liffey agreed.

When they had finished their cereal bars and bottled water, Robert Rivers opened his backpack and took out a small camcorder.

"Daddy, I don't think we can get any good shots from way up here. Maybe closer to the bottom would be better?"

"Liffey, I have a tape for you to watch. I wanted you to view it from the top of the world in a beautiful place. Your mother wanted you to see it when you turned thirteen." "Mother?" Liffey was perplexed. Her mother had been dead for over ten years now.

"Your mother left you a videotape, Liffey. She wanted to say things to you she knew she would not be able to say to a three-year-old little girl," Robert Rivers said, trying his best to remain upbeat and not show Liffey how devastated he still was by her mother's untimely death.

Liffey tried *her* best not to show her father how totally freaked out she was by this soon-to-be-viewed videotape from the *grave*. She did not know *how* to feel about it and was apprehensive about seeing her mother *alive* on videotape after she would have actually been dead for such a long time. Liffey could tell this meant a lot to her father, however, so she braced herself and said, "O.K., Daddy."

Robert Rivers pressed 'play' and Maeve Rivers was instantly there with them on top of Knocknarea. Maeve did not speak immediately. She smiled for a long time into the camera. She was wearing a rust-colored sweater that made her auburn hair look unearthly beautiful. She twirled her pinky finger around her bangs like she was trying to find the right words to say. She then folded her hands together and placed them formally on what Liffey thought was their dining room table.

It was then that Liffey noticed the necklace. It had an 'M' made up of tiny diamonds, like Queen Anne Boleyn's necklace had the ornate 'B' in the painting at the National Portrait Gallery in London.

Maeve Rivers began to speak in a rich, silky voice. Her first words were: "I love you, Liffey. I wish I could be there with you and your daddy right now. But I can't, so here I am in this videotape!"

Liffey pressed 'pause' and gave her father a bewildered look.

"Liffey, if this is too much for you, we don't have to watch it now," her father said gently. "Maybe I should have prepared you for it first."

"Daddy," Liffey said quietly. "The lady in this tape is *not* my mother."

"Denial, classic denial," thought Robert Rivers frantically.

He had not prepared himself at *all* for this reaction. He would have to say something intelligent and quickly but words failed him. All he could say was: "Liffey, honey, I was married to your mother for fifteen years. The lady in this tape *is* your mother. What in the world makes you think she is *not* your mother, Liffey?"

Liffey answered her father matter-of-factly, without any display of emotion. "Because I sat in the seat right next to the lady in this tape on the plane from Pittsburgh to Seattle two years ago, Daddy."

***

PRESS RELEASE
BUCKINGHAM PALACE

A spokesman for The National Portrait Gallery in London has confirmed that the Crowning Portrait of Queen Elizabeth I had been briefly stolen, but is at this very moment safely homeward bound. Her majesty wishes to express her gratitude to a brave and brilliant young American girl, who wishes to remain anonymous.

The End
www.liffeyrivers.com

Made in the USA
San Bernardino, CA
16 August 2014